"THE
CROW'S CRY"

Anastasia Shmaryan

Order this book online at www.trafford.com
or email orders@trafford.com

Most Trafford titles are also available at major online book retailers.

Printed in the United States of America.

ISBN: 978-1-4907-1809-5 (sc)
ISBN: 978-1-4907-1810-1 (e)

Trafford rev. 10/31/2013

North America & international
toll-free: 1 888 232 4444 (USA & Canada)
fax: 812 355 4082

PART I

CHAPTER 1

A crow's cry is airborne; given that its eyes sense something. Next the crow is landing on tree's branch, whereas it slants from the lodge.

Meet the end of day outskirt of an industrial metropolitan area in Detroit. View that general public is returning home from a hard working day.

Here came into sight a typical American home of middle-class ancestors from the third generation of European nomads. This is, where the Lipinski family unit to be found.

In the kitchen is spotting scrawls, lies down of local stats from 'The Daily' newspaper. Among the Lipinski came into the view a man, Peter in his mid-crisis, or being in the age of mid or late forties. He is roughly 1 m 80 cm height; brunette, with grey eyes, and dressed smart. Peter is a wage earner for the Lipinski family. Saw on the opposite side from him stood his wife Rosalyn, a woman in her early or mid-forties. Her color is blond, and probably does dye her hair in saloons not as often as she's being supposed to. Apart from this married pair views their kids: Robert is fourteen-year-old; and their youngest daughter, Sarah-Jane. Alongside, here also came into view an old lady, Margie, who is grandmother to those kids?

Suddenly Peter breaks the news, affirms that wishes split-up from the family: 'I met a woman, younger than me! She has attracted me. So, we have got involved, and continued our relationship! I have fallen in love with her . . .'—Peter inhales; bows head down; given that he delays, as it seems he is tolerably ashamed, but without regrets. Rosalyn on the contrary appears be at a complete loss. Peter takes a lungful of air; and has seen to the right, even if he is dull, but spoke slowly: 'Rosy, I am-m . . .'—, he is hesitant; and bows his head down, thus devoid of staring into her eyes. He is shuddering with his limbs, and affirms: 'Look Rosy! We lived together for many years. Now, I realized that I don't love you anymore! I am glad that our kids were born! Still, I feel as man in a full ability, but in no way myself being an old man not at all!'—Peter is discontinued, and breathing deeply; then he tells more: 'As I am longing to be with a woman I truly love!'—Rosalyn in contrast, looks part heartbreaking, and one part jumpy, when she is staring back at her husband in disbelief, what she has just heard. Impulsively she shakes her head; and cries out: 'Peter, what are you saying? I can't believe it?'—Peter cuts her short; even if his head has curved low; he is kept talking: 'I must end this one and for all! Sorry, Rosy, but I decided to leave you're all . . .'—Seeing her eyes wide-open; as she reacts with a query: 'Just tell me, Peter is it my fault? Since from the day we have met, I always loved you! Married you! Born your kids? Now, what we obliged to split on what basis that our relationship be ruined and for what?'—But he disrupts her: 'I can't take it anymore! Rosy, our kids practically all grown up! Rob predominantly, he will be a great help to all of you're!'—Rosalyn began sobbing, at the same time as she is held a hand lied on her mid size flip-sides; and she appears being an amiable woman; view as tears are rolling down her round cheeks.

At the same very moment kitchen enters Rob. When he saw Rosalyn was upset with damp eyes, and weeping terribly. Thus, Rob resultant to tackle Peter, despite him being confused:

'What is going on in here? Mom, why you're crying?'—
Rosalyn raises her head, but is on edge; next she looks at her
husband: 'Son, it would be better if your dad tells you alone all
about it?'—Each of the adults is tacit: but Peter break a dead
silent, is meaning: 'Rob, it's not easy for me to say this, but I am
leaving all of you are. For the reason that I need some time to
be alone. I am sorry, son . . .'—He gets interrupted by Robert
that, looks distress to cry: 'Why, dad? Have I done something
awful?'—On a critical point Robert is begun panting.

On impulse the teenager starts fleeing the room, just as he is
expressing grief on the way.

More than two hours have past since Rob shut himself in the
bathroom, is emerged sitting on the floor and held hands up on
his forehead. Like so Rob has expressed grief that, lest it function
in between breathing, seen his shoulders trembled.

In the corridor, meanwhile, is seeing the Lipinski, accompanied
by Sarah-Jane and Margie, having marched, as their echoes being
heard? This old lady appears pale and frail, while she is crying.
Yet this lady senior is calling for her grandson, by way of being
prayerful: 'Robert, sweetie I beg you, please, open the door! It's

already have past dinnertime. But you didn't even touch your food?'—Seen Peter is upset, while tensely tugs his earlobe; next he deals with his son, except is edgy: 'Rob, are you in there? Just tell us? Your mom and I were worried about you, son?'-

For the time being Rob shed tears, and sound of his voice came back in horse pitches: 'No! I won't come out!'—This teenager is kept crying, gasping for air, then he stated: 'If dad swears that he's going to stay with us?'—On the spot Peter shakes his head: 'Look, Rob I don't wish to deceive you! But if you promise to come out, I give my word we will get to talk!'—

All the Lipinski is standing at the entry and look at each-other, and nod with their heads. Saw shoulders of the adults' move up and down, but they are breathless. Rob listen cagily, next declares in a shaky voice: 'Okay, dad! I am coming out!'-

When the door gets slowly open, there appears first Rob's head in the entry, followed by his slim complexion that is slowly crawling in. Rob gave the impression of being one part scared and one part sad; seen that tears is fixed in his eyes. Suddenly Peter takes hold of his left hand, and is explaining: 'Rob you must know: your mother and I have talked about . . .'—As eye contacted has made by Peter with Rosalyn, but he is unrelenting:

'I will come often to visit you and Sarah-Jane, essentially when both of your school holidays are coming up. The three of us can spend time together. I will take you and Sarah traveling to Beach in Mexico!'—But Rob prevents him from talking, when cries out: 'Dad, you're liar! I don't want you to leave! I love you, daddy! Don't leave me, please!'—Given Peter holds Rob's hand that, teen tries, and is freeing himself from hanged off dad's stiff grasp.

On impulse the teenager flees the room, where he disappears behind the ingress . . .

Long times pass since Rob has run away. Seen in the house each among the Lipinski is looking worried for Rob's well-being. Rosalyn who is first breaking silent, when argues with Peter: 'This is your entire fault! Where would Robert can hide?'—

On the spot their daughter, Sarah-Jane intrudes into the argument: 'Mom, dad, I know where Rob is?'—Now the adults turn attention to their youngest daughter. Wisely Peter's head is curved down; when he asks: 'Sarah, do you really know, where he is? Just tell us?'—And Sarah-Jane is drawn in, telling: 'Rob is up in the attic, playing guitar!'—By hearing it, they became inquisitive: 'Are you sure, Sarah? How do you know that?'—She puts in the picture for them: 'Cause, when Robert has problems, from time to time he goes up to attics . . .'—Peter then spins to face his wife, and suggests to:—Rosy, come up quick, than over?'—Rosalyn exhales; takes aback and agrees: 'Okay, then! Let's go up there?'—Given that Sarah-Jane is following them. Ensuing Rosalyn is angled; and sees to her: 'Where do you think you're going young lady? I didn't say-so? Sarah, better go in your room and try to sleep! We will talk to Rob without your help!'— Here Sarah-Jane is naïvely decisive: 'Okay, mommy! Good night, Daddy!'—Peter is hesitant, thus he's uneasy: 'All right, Sarah-Jane! Good night too you to! Now, go to sleep, sweetheart!'-

This trio of adults plus Margie has left the room . . .

A buzz inflates, and is heard rhythm of Rob's heartbeat.

Seen the Lipinski is walking; next climbing up and slowly progressing, where echoes of their footsteps being heard outer walls from the stairs; with the aim to reach Rob in attics. In attics saw cobwebs, which hanged over; and is covered in dust randomly with rusty round. In premises is vision of gloomy, only light came from a window that hasn't been cleaned for ages. From all sides be heard sound of doves, or other birds are on the wing being following those echoes.

Out off walls hatches the way and is leading to a solid door that gets open, where up-and-coming the Lipinski trio, with Margie counted too. Saw tears fixed in her eyes, when she has risen her voice; but it is tender: 'Robert, dear, where are you? You haven't done schooling for tomorrow?'—Next in line is Rosalyn, who tried being cool, calm and collected; yet she is jumpy: 'Robert! I know you in there! As we have heard you're sniffing?'—While resonance of her voice being heard through empty walls. So far, rhythm of Robert's breathing is improved. Disparity from Rosalyn's face vanished; her feet are in motion; next she stops near an old cask. There are hearing those footsteps advance, as thumping the stone floor; this is Peter's shoes that be well-known to Rob. Peter looks be annoyed: 'So, Rob you still refuse to come out?'—Next in line Margie who is weeping, seeing her shoulders is shaken: 'Robert dear, please show your face?'—Still hearing as Margie is crying. Rosalyn is taken lungful of air. Peter's face turns green is of fuming; even as he resolutely disrupts Rosalyn, decides single handled his son; and tells him: 'Rob you always 'do whatever you like? That is enough! It's time to take radical measures! I will grab him, and drag out 'from this bloody attic!'-

Due to teen's sensation, first his heart plunges; resultant it's begun functioning in normal rhythms; still booms being heard. Peter bears, and butts in, but is disappointed. Next is hearing he began yelling bitterly and repeatedly: 'Rob, do you hear me? Come out, immediately!'—All at once feels that Rob's heart began functioning in a normal beat. Just then Peter proclaims: 'Rob, come on down! Or you will be banned for a month! Unless, I won't come to visit you and Sarah, when both of your school holidays coming up! Cause the three of us can spend time being together, I will take you and Sarah traveling with me to the Mexican beach.'—Seen him, Peter rudely clings to his hand. But Robert is freed from his dad's stiff grasp; he then be set in motion. Just then saw Robert flees the loft; and is vanished into the night?

Meanwhile, its start of a nervy match amid adults: given that Peter clatters with his worn shoes over the stone-floor, with a growl. Margie is crying. Rosalyn is like a crazy disrupting everyone. On the spot amidst those occurs a nervy lump there.

11

Over the splitting between Rob's parents, which he has taken with difficulty, as struggles to accept.

Next came their divorce that hits harder on this teenager to handle it.

So far in his life, Robert feels being alone, equally is forlorn too. Due to what have resulted from his parents split; he would spend free time being on his own. Given that Rob has excess to the upstairs room, into attics.

CHAPTER 2

It's a purple sunrise, where across be able to see title of the High School, in Detroit.

At the present in school see those pupils from grade seven. They are fourteen years of age, as having seated at the tables in classroom, and listen to a mature teacher, Miss Hostler, who gave a speech for them.

From know where one of these pupils spits out a chewing gum that has flown from a tube up-front. Gum trails; then hits Robert on the back of his head, as a result it caused him ghastly pain; and he shrieks out. To investigate Lipinski spins around to look at that class of pupils, where seem the two familiar faces laughing their heads off, they are Martin McDermott, fourteen; and another teenager the same age as the former that, is seated beside Martin, whose name Jonah van de Borg. Robert is naïve, and doesn't have a clue, which caused him such ghastly pain. Resultant that Rob is yelling: 'Ouch! Who spat out in my neck? Would you do it? Dudes just tell, who of you are seen it?'—Jonah be heated, and reacts: 'Shut up, you idiot! Don't disrupt the class!'—Here also sees the teacher's whose name Miss Hostler that stood at the heart of a classroom, when she stops him. Though mood among the pupils are soaring. Next this teacher embarks on Rob, is forceful: 'So, Lipinski, it is you, who disrupted the lesson?'—She looks into his eyes, is displeased. Just as Robert became silent, she is prying: 'What this time happened, Lipinski? With whom now you on bad terms?'—When Hostler turns to face the whole class; at the same time she became lucid without paying attention to Rob, but is firm and loud: 'Now, all of you're, listen and be aware! Tomorrow you will have to sit for physics exams! I insist that all of you're looking in the textbooks 'so as not to be surprised with the question papers I prepared for you are . . .'—

At this time seen in the school workshop near a stand those groups of youths, who are talking to the male teacher. Teacher's name is Hugo Morales, who being supposed to instruct pupils with designs that proper for carpentry or other skills, which employs for line of machinery. Seen on the table be arranged a whole set full with tools, amid that include a drill. Hugo keys up and explains: 'So, boys and girls! Listen and watch how the woodwork proceeds.'-

This way twenty minutes pass. Those circled pupils dutifully have studied. Next they are given a task to selecting for their own future professions. Among those three, who Hugo chosen are supposed to showcase to others their knowledge in has selected: 'Now Lipinski, George and Cheryl will demonstrate for all of us, how they create their own designs? They would apply planes that are to be used by them to shave woods with it . . .'—

The moment Rob took in his hand planes is fixated on shaving woods, while he works it out so as to create objects.

A sudden person destructed Rob, when a piece of metal has thrown at him that hits his arm. On the spot Rob turns his head from side to side, which is caused harm to his right hand from the tool. As results of a knock he began bleeding profusely: 'Ouch! It hurts! Mister Morales, can you see blood is pouring from my wound!'—Next Rob is thrown a tool out of his hand that it's fallen on the ground. On the spot Hugo became worried, when saw the boy is bleeding. So, he grabs Rob's wounded hand; but struggles to stop blood pouring on teen's wrist.

These rest of pupils have reacted being troubled with this accident. While amidst few with Martin counting, seem is amused off that stir. He uproars, when has thrown steel stick at Rob, who is naïve, and doesn't discern; if any were with abhor towards him.

Later a nurse turns up there; and has worked on Rob's wound by dressing it. Equal he takes hold of it, but Rob is yelling from an awful pain.

CHAPTER 3

The next day, the moment Robert came home from school; after he has eaten late lunch. Rob then let Rosalyn know: 'Mom, I am going to attics!'—Rosalyn spins in front to face her son, with a curious look, but of fret, saw to: 'Robert, what about your studies?'—As Rob gets up of his sit; and is ready to run off somewhere, even if he looks forlorn. She bows her head down, and points of his injured hand: 'I need to do on your hand a fresh dressing?'—Echo of her voice is flowing, and it vanished in the air. As a self-rule Rob doesn't pay attention to her, after he opens the front door, and wanes . . .

Rob is seated in attics for a while. While he is begun reminiscence that, overwhelmed his mind . . .

With this memory that avalanche, Rob began to remember, what the teacher has told the class earlier today in school. Being naive to realize that some would listen, Rob talks to himself: 'What I am going to do? Dad is not with us any longer! Will any help me practice for the exams? I can bet that I will fail test in physics, tomorrow?'-

At this point from nowhere Rob began hearing wing is airborne; then it slams, like the birds have flown in.

Out of the blue, a timbre round of a bird is on the wings, next hearing a crow's cry: 'Kar-kar-kar!'-

Rob at once moves up his head, where it appears the crow that has mixture of green in its eyes that, is staring at him from above. Seen the crow is witty; and it's fond, of what this boy's thoughts are. Next the crow angles, as soaring across. For that reason the teen exclaims, is panic-stricken: 'Oh!'—Then the crow croaks, appear it thinks at first, seems it came to like Rob. After the bird slants down, and is landing fast; seen as uses its paw, while gets to hold on the windowsill.

At first this teen is afraid: 'A bird? It's a crow! Gosh! Shush! That's what I don't need now! Get the hell away, where you come from! My life is a living hell without you, bloody crow!'—Except for a crow's reaction, it is with a croak: 'Kar!'-

Even if Rob starts to scare off the magpie wags hand absolutely not, in its place is sitting still on a window frame. Now be spotted that crow's eyes sharp, but mixed with bog-yellow nuance, as it has stared at Rob, who is scared. Rob glances through, laid-back as his head with shoulders are shaken. Since encounter with a bird turns impulsive, Rob is intrigued; just as he speaks, smirks: 'You're bloody peril or you not, crow? Shush! Fly away, Goddamn! Get the hell out! Leave me alone!'—The crow croaks, like gave him a hint: 'Kar-Kar-Kar!'-

In attics is murky, minus window is foggy, thus Rob couldn't see well. So, Rob's frown his eyes, and watches the crow that turns out being a magpie. This teen can tell apart that it's a magpie: on low backs of bird's wings is shown white tips that enclosed plume. Rob is seemingly confused: 'Okay! No games today! Shush! I have more things to worry about instead to play! Cause tomorrow I am sitting for exams in school! Thus, I am in a shitty mood!'—Robert smirks; at once he turns ruthless: 'Your sharp crow's eye are able sensing stuffs, as well to find corpses, don't you? Are you hungry, crow?'—The crow croaks, whereas its echo is heard on all sides: 'Kar-kar-kar!'-

Robert has found leftovers that brought up before.

Once he has placed down a container half-full of meals; the bird with no timid as the crow soars, is landing with its paws down on the ground. Then the magpie starts to chew it. Seen Rob is content: 'At least someone is pleased? If I can only have wings as you bird I would fly to pick up notes elsewhere? Or I will fail the exams tomorrow! Yes!'-

A sudden magpie began timbre around is baiting with crash of bird wings that being heard. After circling over ceiling, the magpie is flown away.

CHAPTER 4

It seems is a fine crack of dawn in Detroit. Here, comes into sight an empty storeroom, where indoor are appearing those two teenagers deep in writing crib-notes on long pieces of paper. This is Martin McDermott in lead; on opposite side sits his mate, Jonah Van de Borg, and being at the same age, as he is.

On a whim the doorway gets opened, while strong winds start to blow in that caused the window swing; eventually it gets wide open.

Bolt from the blue, seen a bird flew in storage is made chaos, and the crow cries: 'Kar-Kar-Kar!'-

Unless those youths are scared; given both as one get out of seat them being in motion towards exit.

The bird is flying just now, where it has circled twice over ceiling. The bird is soaring; as has resultant landed with mitt;

touches on the surface of a desk, where those Schoolboys were seated a minute ago. When the magpie opens its beak, and start-pecking crib-notes, like it is ready to have a feast. Given that bird is seized robustly pieces of writing employing its beak; then puts them in its jaws. Once the work was completed; the magpie without delay has baited, been swaying with its wings, yet again made chaos: 'Kar!'—The crow soars with no timid; after it has winged across a window the bird is flown away, who knows where too?

With crow's disappearance, those schoolboys seem are dazed, but shaken; seen they kept freeze, from what having occurred a minute ago. Only then Martin starts talking to his buddy, Van de Borg hears, as his voice is shaky: 'Jonah, do you have a clue, what just have happened?'—Jonah bows his head, but he still is scared: 'Not really? When I saw a crow that flew in here, and I almost did in my pants!'-

Those youths are looking at each other, and panicky be written in their eyes. On the spot Jonah clarifies: 'I wouldn't know how a Goddamn crow be able to fly in?'—Martin's defiance is ferocious: 'Look, who the hell does need to know about a bloody crow? We must worry about the upcoming exams! Do you know if everyone keeps cribs?'—Before Jonah is raring for the exit, he discloses to Martin: 'I know just one, who's having crib-notes for a few years?'—At that moment Jonah the pupil, is drawn near Martin; and begun whispering into his ear: 'Don't worry about it, Martin. I will call Kuhn's from grade eleven, and ask him to bring crib-notes in here. Do you think he still has it?'—But Martin is tricky: 'I think he does! Here you go, and do it faster!'-

At the same morning Rob is walking to school through a thick snowfall. Before entering entry of the main building; a crow is flying over Robert's head, and by it a quick throw down at him pieces of script. View it is a magpie that flew, when it has thrown papers down on his head from above. Saw as the bird is away; while a minute ago it has brought crib-notes. Out of respects, Rob smirks on a lucky occasion; and talks to himself: 'Gosh, I am in luck! Now I know that I will do well in exams?'-

Already in the classroom Rob is writing on a note pad, where sitting next to a girl. There he is focused on question paper. There are hearing voices, where the teacher has proceeded with lecturing those pupils. This is Miss Hostler that declared: 'Now, I order the class set to question papers!'—

Those pupils have got pre-occupied by way of overwriting in their aimed themes; per head in the midst of class all of them are overpoweringly into the exams, but unmoved.

Here at least twenty minutes pass, seen in the heart of classroom amid the pupils who have written dotty about sessions, with what they are doing? Rob meantime, sits, but being occupied by peeking into crib-notes, and challenges the question papers.

Sees at the heart of class, in reserve of the pupils are standing Hostler, who attentively checks on their progress, which have got deep into writing examinations. On the spot the teacher comes close to Rob, without him hearing her footsteps. Bending over him she is seized Rob's hand, as recklessly tilts up, while in her other hand held crib-notes; sees she is shaking tiny papers up in the air. Next she says publicly is ironic: 'Lipinski, what in hell you're doing? Who gave you the rights cheating on the exam?'— Rob looks one part alarmed one part lost; seen his upper arms shyly shaking, when he is reacting: 'Miss Hostler, let me explain to you, please . . .'—But she stops him; she then turns to look at the pupils, and be firm: 'Shut up, Lipinski!'—Hostler takes her reading glasses off; she then wipes lenses with intents to order the pupils to be quiet. She then spins around to face class. She makes public by hustles to them with ample of Rob's slip, when looks in his eyes, is yelling: 'All of you are, listen carefully! Who else have brought the crib-notes? In case, if you did? You like him will bear the consequences! Now, all continue with exams!'—Hostler turns to Rob, handles him; hear her be annoyed: 'Now, Robert, do come with me!'-

Once Hostler has exited classroom, Rob is following her seems him being ashamed and panicky. Once she is closed the door behind, she then grabs Rob's hand, and says firm: 'Now, Lipinski, go in detention! And wait for the Head Master to take in his hand your case? But, do not forget to bring your parents to be present? Go, pronto . . .'—

Soon after came end of examinations that be held in the assembly, and where those pupils have set for . . .

Later on Hostler came to the room, where Rob being kept in detention: 'Have you talked to Head Master yet, Lipinski?'— While Robert is seemingly sad: 'Yes Miss Hostler! Please, let me 'explain crib-notes don't belong to me! I have no idea how these pieces ended up with me? A crow was flying around, when it has thrown pieces of paper down on my head . . .'—Rob hasn't done explaining, when he's being disrupted by Hostler, who is sulk; seen her head inclines: 'Mister Lipinski, do you really think I was born yesterday?'—On the spot he is begun talking in a diplomatic manner: 'No! Believe me, Miss Hostler I am telling you the truth! And, I am begging you, Miss, please, allow me to finish the exams?'-

Rob makes his way across the school vestibule.

Next he came quick to where is separated patterns in lines that are hanged in between overcoats and various sizes of jackets to be seen there. At this point has become spectacle for him. Given that Rob is scared, while those few pupils chased after him, among who are spotting Martin and Jonah. Lastly Rob found a place to hide within the patterns, where those teens somehow are having walked on him. On the spot they began dragging him away, just as Rob is trying to twist his arm out to free himself off those teens rough hands. Though Martin looks be annoyed: 'You idiot, Rob! How did our cribs endued in your hands? These pieces couldn't run alone in the street?' Rob is panicky, hearing as his tone of voice is shaky: 'No! But, I have nor idea dudes!'-

Despite his resistance and cry out for help, those teens cruelly have taken hold of Rob's collar; then together they are dragging him to the end of line. On a whim Rob has grown savage; is getting hold to one of hanged hooks by; but of late loses clash . . .

Soon the door of a teacher's room opened, and on a threshold here was Hugo. He ran at once towards the teens, which are at each other throats. Morales saw as Rob running from that gang; and in a difficult situation he gets at once into their clash; seems he's being heated, on the spot covers up Rob with his bulky figure: 'Hey! Whoa, you're dudes! Stop it! What's seems to be the problem?'— But Martin reacts, by gnashing his teeth: 'He is an idiot, and a thief!'—Rob is miserable, and says smugly: 'I am not a thief! I did not steal anything from anyone! And when my dad comes to school; he will show his muscle to all of you're, dudes . . .'—But Hugo stops him, when says firmly: 'That's enough stop it, all of you! Dudes let me give you're a piece of advice: if you all want to be dismissed from school? Go on hold this stupid fight . . .'—

When all has been settled, those teens are on track of walking off. Prior to exit, Martin spins facing Rob, and is holding his fist up. Though he's being madly against Rob, like so, he speaks in a vulgar:

'Robby-booby you lucky this time? Next time you 'won't be so . . .'—But, Morales is disrupted him it seems being in his effort of counseling: 'McDermott and you Jonah, get the hell out from here! Before I change my mind about you're two, and I report of your gang to the Head Master of your clash, which have happened in the past few minutes! . . .'—

Once those teens have left, Hugo is begun a chat with Robert: 'Lipinski, don't pay heed to these dudes! Just tell me the truth, what Martin was talking about that you have stolen some stuff? What was that?'—Rob bows his head down; takes breaths, as is deep in thoughts, but he says sadly: 'Mister Morales as I have said, I did not steal a thing! He talked about crib-notes that I used, when Miss Hostler has caught me on the exams?'—Now Hugo is shocked: 'Rob I haven't anticipated that you will cheat on the exams? Where did you get cribs in the first place?'—Rob inhales; looks him in the eyes, and is mumbling frankly: 'Mister Morales, in the Morning when I was walking to school, a crow flew from nowhere, and thrown crib-notes down on my head. Don't look at me, like I am an idiot? I am telling the truth, I swear it!'—Hugo is dazed, but his shoulders shivered: 'Seem to be Rob that maybe . . .

'In my practice won't know what I will believe in?

Just tell me, if crib-notes were yours?'—But Rob reacts, as is shaken with his head:' No! And I do not know, whom these crib-notes belonged to, sir?'-

Like this some minutes pass. Hugo who is first breaking the dead silence, and talks gently: 'Listen, dude, I know why you're upset, but arguing just now with those boys? Cause people having good days and bad! Today you're, Robert being unlucky . . . 'Rob, who is shyly, but oddly looks at him, and disrupts: 'Mister Morales, were you too getting divorced?'—Now the teacher is displeased, and stares at Rob, by saying: 'Lipinski, what do you mean 'You to getting divorce'? You will be doing some explanation?'—Rob is nervy: 'I'm sorry Mister Morales, I talked about my folks. Dad has left us! Now my parents in the process of divorce! But I do not want it! I wish dad had stayed with us always?'—Teacher looks at him with regrets. He then is patted teen's head, telling gently: 'Rob, don't worry about a thing! And don't be hard on yourself? Now I get it why you failed the studies?'

Abruptly Hugo is changed the course, and he's sound rather positively: 'A while ago on my lesson, I saw you have worked and ideally applied planes on shaved woods! Else you were operating on the machinery near perfect, and grind metals well!'—Rob spins facing the teacher, as seems is agreeable: 'Mister Morales is it true? Do you really think that 'I did well on your lessons?'-, Hugo winks to him: No doubts about it, Rob! As in the real world you can do well with learning, by and large how to develop into a joiner?—Rob smirks: 'Can I come too, Mister Morales? I am not awfully eager to be a joiner, but it would-be handy to build stuff?'—Hugo likes this beams; nods he's head, and is telling:— You know Rob after school hours in a workshop I give lesson for those, who want to gain skills and develop into joiners? Why don't you come too!'—Rob looks with interest to the teacher: 'Sir, I like this idea, but I am afraid if mom finds out, gosh I will get in trouble!'—Here Hugo winks at him; that ducks his head up and down: 'Don't worry about that! I will talk to your mom, and get her consent.

'Hereafter, you can call me Hugo! Okay, Robert?'-

CHAPTER 5

O ver three months have past. Here it is after Midday, as the pupils have ended studies in school.

Outwardly in someone's backyard are hearing instruments playing a tune. Rob is walking, and has worn guitar-case that hung up on his flipside. Rob peeks an access to storage; next he bravely opens the front door, and has crossed the threshold. In there he has spotted a young band is playing and singing. Since Rob lacks firstly to sense, it does feel a strong smell, given someone has smoked marijuana or similar stuff that, he is observed; and been suspicion. Resultant Rob freezes, and bows his head down. On the spot he sees in the mirror a few of his classmates'; amid them is Martin, when brings to halt the band in performance; that he too is fixed his eyes on Rob. Though Martin gave those signs to cut off; next he is yelling: 'Hey dudes, stop it! Fellas cut

31

off!'—He shows sign: cut the neck; and he is recurring: 'Dudes, stop it! Cut 'off!'—Then Martin turns to face Rob, in a critical point his face altered, hands up and he is shaking a knuckle. But his tongue is in cheek: 'Look dudes this is what I found? What in hell are you doing here, Rob?'—Rob is timid, but afraid: 'A rumor has it that you set up a band? I was tipped to come here and join you are?'—Jonah, who exposes, prevents him: 'So if we are? What's to you dickhead? Or maybe you're spying on us?'—Hearing that blame Rob is fearful, when he turns toward the door, being ready to run. But Jonah and one more teen are jumped in front of Rob, and tries byline of attack to cut off his exit. Then they have pushed Robert off. Seen Rob falls down into the stony ground. Smack! One more smack! Be one punch! Then, a second punch! Ouch! Ensuing Martin rips off Robert's hands the guitar, and drops the instrument, and is begun smashing it down into the ground. Given Rob's guitar has got broken down in half that lies on the ground. It follows that Rob looks terrified: 'Stop it! Why did you desperate to break my guitar? This was a gift from my dad!'—Jonah gives a push onto Rob's upper arm, just as he has tried to run off. Whilst another teen jump in, even as these rest of them are in motion, which having sized, and they twist Rob's hand backside. With line of attack

Jonah is trying to cut off Rob's exit; and deviously: 'Where do you think you're going?'—Here Martin is cynical: 'Were you played your-guitar? Now you don't, dumber!'—Stupidly he prevents Rob from saying; equally is ironic: 'You stupid, who gives a toss about your guitar? I know you saw us smoking stuff? If you came to spy on us and tell anyone?'-, Rob cuts him short; but he is scared: 'No, dudes! I won't tell a soul! I didn't see that you were smoking! Dudes, it's not my business anyway? Who does what, days and where on?'-

Next saw Jonah turns to the door where Kuhn is standing and steps in front; as he points to: 'Kuhn, open the window? Let's make a foggy smell to vanish it on outside? Do it!'—On a critical point Martin breaks in, holds a knuckle up be influentially mad: 'Listen, you dickhead! Did you see us smoking marijuana? Did you not Rob?'—In a difficult situation Rob is panicky, thus has said in shaky voice: 'No! I came here to join the band! Dudes, I am telling you are the truth!'

After Martin spins in front of them; it looks as if he is furious: 'Dudes, do we trust this dickhead? No! If we let him go he opens his big mouth, and tells someone? Will he sell us out? Yes! Come on dudes! Show him, what he needs to forget? Let's get him!'— Martin toughly jumps atop of Rob, and hits him. Seen the rest of those guys following, are getting tough on Rob weakness. Smack! Punch! One of them blows a second punch! Ouch! But he attempts resist that gang; and tries to hold on. Martin is mad, and aver in rage: 'Rob, you're dickhead! Will I show you how to steal note?'—On the spot Rob is scared, and offended: 'I didn't steal it! I swear!'—Martin is still fumed, while he makes eyes contact with those dudes: 'Rob, if you tell anyone, what you saw we will make your life like an instrument Hell!'—Then and there Robert is crying for help on top of his lungs: 'Let me go! Help! Help me, somebody!'—Those guys separately are kept hitting him over his body; be caused by it Rob lies down on the ground. Cogently Martin is led a gang, which's caused: him harshly twisting Rob's elbow.

All at once a crow cries over; then it is flown in through an open window. The magpie is soaring, once it descents, and takes on that gang. Next the bird lands atop of Martin's head, and covers him around with its wing. Saw crow's bog-yellow eyes stare at Martin, who is afraid? On the spot the crow strikes with a sharp beak in Martin's eye; then it draws to halt. Now the bird hits him in forehead, then in his face. Martin began yelling from a shock and pain: 'Ouch! Dudes, help me? Get the Hell this fucking 'crow away from me! Ouch! It hurts! Somebody, help!'-

In a flash Martin distant himself from those. Given that gang by now have frozen and stopped attacking Rob, as they're hesitating being scared to approach the crow. Seen Martin has covered his injured eye with one hand, with his free hand is attempted to push away the crow. Martin roars, while his hands in the air waving: 'I will kill you're bloody crow! Shush! Dudes, catch this Goddamn bird! Knock this fucking crow down! Hey, guys get closer to the bird, do a jump, and 'grab by its wings!'—Except for magpie is swaying with its wing, then goes up in the air, as made chaos around? The rest of that gang is scared, of which caused Martin's wounds, as he state of health have worsen. Since it's flying around ceiling, the guys are jumping, and attempting to catch the crow.

While Rob is back up on his feet; and sees a chance to move towards exit. Prior to leave Rob waves hand up, since the bird is airborne; he is winced so as to warn the magpie: 'Hey, Gale, fly away! Faster!'-

Coming on open-air Robert is kept running, passing through backyard, then athwart 100 yards. He only stops to suck in air; seems he is in high spirits.

Briefly Rob began recalling, how those boys have offended him a lot. Abruptly he comes back to reality: what he has learned by rote. In that case Rob puts a smile; talks to himself, but be sadden:

'Those guys have often hurt me! If it wasn't for my Crow I don't know what might happen with me? Gale is a savior . . .'— He thinks for a tad; puts a smile, as it's struck him: 'Yes, I can call the crow Gale! If it was not for my bird, I don't know, what might 'happen there? Thanks to Gale that flew in the right place, and in the right time!'-

Meet lovely daylight of anew day, outskirts of Detroit. There came into the sight Rob who ran, and attempts to matching magpie, which is flying. Next Rob stops; and turns around to observe the field. Raising his head up Rob is thriving with joy: 'Wait for me, Gale!'—This crow is reacting with: 'Kar!'-

In split seconds the magpie flew toward Rob; and it is speedily landing down on a tree's branch, just above his head. Seen Rob is carefree: 'Gale, come down! Land here, up on my arm? Do you know that I am talking?'—He hasn't finished saying, while the bird flown down on him; it advances by descending, next is landing onto this teenager's armrest.

CHAPTER 6

Since a friendship began between the lad and a magpie, over a year pass by. At this time of the year is winter; seen on the outside is coating with snow-white and it's wintry weather. Despite of a frosty climate, there is a beautiful and sunny day.

Now, in the school hallway be hanged a poster for the upcoming Christmas, and New Year celebration.

Given that Rob stood aside, while Rosalyn and Peter are talking to Hostler, who is saying unpleasant things about Rob: '. . . I am sorry, but your son has a stubborn nature! So, I advise you are considering placing Rob in specially guardian school, where he will be getting help . . .'—Rosalyn prevents her from saying more: 'What are you talking about? My son is in good physical health, equally and mentally!'—This lady-teacher has a word again: 'What about your son's deeds, for instance, lately 'he stole somewhere crib-notes, and was cheating on my exam? How about that?'-

In a critical point Rob intruded, seems he is shamed: 'Mom, have I ever stole anything?'—Follows that Rosalyn turns to look at Peter, and became upset; then she lays blame, on him: 'Peter, its your entire fault? If you haven't left us for a Bimbo, this would never happen with Robert?'—Peter feels not be wicked; that he reacts upon it: 'Rosy, this is not the place for you to spill the beans . . .'—

Suddenly Hugo has approached the quartet; there he sees: Rosalyn is distressed to cry. On impulse Morales tackles Hostler: 'Excuse me, what is going on between you all? Miss Hostler, why they are all upset?'—He looks aside at Rosalyn; by his turn away, he then is pointing towards Robert . . .

Soon after Peter has left, Hugo turns attention to Rosalyn, yet again: 'Mrs. Lipinski, listen, do not get upset about Robert. I can assure you that your son is a fine and talented young man!'—She still appears distressed, and yet she raised her head up: 'Thank you. Are you Rob's teacher too?'—Hugo nods his head. In that case she subsides: 'What is your name?'—He beams, and looks

at her shyly: 'My name is Hugo, do you remember me? Can I
'call you Rosy?'—At once she puts a smile: 'Yes you can, I do
recall . . .'—He stops her; takes breathes, and speaks his mind:
'Rosalyn, can I tempt you to go with me in the Café? . . .'—

In this way times pass by. Rob is sitting in his house, whereas
at the table doing schoolwork. On other side on the couch, sits his
younger sister Sarah-Jane that is reading a book there.

Suddenly the door gets open, whereas on the entry appears
Rosalyn is walking in; a tag along is Hugo Morales. When the
children turn their heads toward entrance, they became silence.
Their mother appears cheerful, and without delay starts reporting
to the kids: 'Children I hope you don't mind that I invited Mister
Morales to spend Christmas and New Year Eve with us?'—Those
kids look at one another, still they seem are at a complete loss.

CHAPTER 7

Like so another year pass. The spring is already arrived in the city. View the sun is shining with its delightful rays. Rob by now has turned sixteen years, whereas he is sitting on the sofa, and reading a book.

Curtly the front door gets open, where shows up Hugo that is walking in alongside Rosalyn. Somewhat seemingly troubles this couple. After chats start between them, when Rosalyn asks: 'Hugo give me advice, what to do?'—Hugo appears is confused: 'Rosy I wish I could?'—Though she wipes tears out of her face: 'Where can I get amount that we owed to the Bank?'—Hearing that Rob grows be at a complete loss. Yet he entails: 'Mom, I want to call dad, and ask for his help?'—Rosalyn turns to face him: 'I don't think so, son. Your dad will rather spend money on this bimbo, Tatiana than helping us? I could bet that he is in somebody's debt?'-

In despair a few hours pass by, sudden the telephone is ringing. Peter gets up of his sit, and be in motion by languor to answer: 'Hello! Peter's speaking!'—He is talking on the telephone, whereas Rob panting in some phone booth. When a man's voice on the phone: 'Hello! Who is this?'—Next Rob is talking boldly: 'Hi, dad! It's me Rob!'—Robert is talking eager on the phone, but panting. Peter responds:' Hi, son!'—Next turn is Rob of talking: 'I am glad that have caught you, dad, although I tried to call you before . . .'—Rob be stopped by Peter, who listens on the line; then his voice is elastic on the phone: 'Okay, son! I need to tell 'you something! Do you remember I promised to take you and Sarah to that beach in Mexico?'—This time Rob listens keenly; seen is in the phone booth, when abruptly he speaks up: 'Yes, Sarah and I waited for that trip! When are we leaving, dad?'—Peter is lazily listening on the phone line; but interrupts his son, when rapidly has said, even if he's voice wary: 'Look! Changes of plans came up, son! Cause of it we must delay our trip, for now! But I promise three of us will go to the Beach, next time!'—Rob's face alters to pale, view spark vanishes from his eyes, while is listening to Peter's retort. In his turn Rob enlightens, but is sadden: 'No? Why shouldn't we travel?'—Hear Peter on the line is taken breaths.

Rob then is talking in pleasing voice: 'Dad I am not calling you about that, but because I need your help? Do you remember that we have mortgage on our house to pay off?'—Peter's tone with sorrow: 'Yes.'—Rob tells more: 'But the Bank ordered us to pay off debts now! If not, the Bank will take over, and we end up live on the road?'—Peter listens, sniffs; he then charily retorts, as seems being gloomy: 'I know, son! But I have problems on my own to deal with! But don't say a word to Sarah! Believe me, if I could, I would help you're all!'—Since Peter on the phone line is panting. By way Rob has listened of what his dad just said; and is reacting crossly: 'Dad you know, Sarah and I sick of your promises! You constantly gave your word, but it was always the same, we are disgusted with your false assurances?'-

In the hours of darkness, Rob comes within reach of his mom and dad's ex-bedroom. When he opens the door: in view Rosalyn be caught unaware that lies next to Hugo under bedding: both of them are half-naked. In a flash Robert became fuming, as a result he is opting; and he flees the room without delay. Rosalyn grows be ashamed, of what has taken place just now. Yet she hops up of bed; then runs after him, on the way her yelling, is jumpy:

'Son, please, wait! Let me explain?'—Hear her voice resound, but it's remained indoors. But Robert is closed the door with a dull sound, after has left.

A few hours pass, since a tension has arisen amid the Lipinski. In front of attic is casing, hung up a poster: "Don't enter!"

Much later: only if Hugo's rough hands are opened a hatch, way in through to attic: and Rob is exposed.

By way of tactics Hugo then grabs Rob's collar, and began dragging this teenager out off his refuge. Meaning of Hugo's voice be heard: 'Why the hell you were hanging around attics? Don't you feel relaxed in your own room? Tell me, Rob?'—Here the teen is well spoken: 'Mister Morales, here I play with bunch of doves! The singing birds help me dreaming! I see the world in unusual light! In here from a window I can view the Great Lakes, and much more! But you have distressed my ally magpie, whom I always bring meals to chew!'—Hugo is on edge: 'Rob, your mom told me that you have stopped studying? All of your free time you're hiding in attics, instead of helping your mom and sister?'— But Rob acts in response with a biting wit: 'You teacher is not my daddy! And, don't give me orders what to do? Your Morales, since you moved in our home, which told you that I approved for you're sleeping with my mom?'—When Hugo hears wicket deed from Rob, he is grown to be tense. On the spot he deals with his stepson: he began dragging Robert close to the exit. Hugo still is upset: 'You're ungrateful little rascal! Don't know that Sarah and you, Rob means the world to me? Like you two my own kids! And I love Rosalyn that is a good thing?'-

CHAPTER 8

It is a superb daytime outside. Here, in the Bank a cashier is counting banknotes. Primary she wraps up, and is packing it; resulting she lies bundle after bundle on shelf. Sees another teller sits inside the glass-sill, and is processing Bank checks. A perceives sound: the phone rang in view of that the Bank manager ran to answer this call.

By next turn the sliding doors open, and Rob is walking in together with Rosalyn. There are two a mother and a son, be joined that queue in the Bank.

With ten minutes go by, as the sliding doors get open, those new clients arrived. View a crow flew in, and follows the customers.

Next the crow flew toward the cashiers, which is amid those seen in her hand, and her being tallying notes. The magpie lands on the counter; then pushes its tiny head into windowsill. In a flash the bird opens its beak, and employs it is attempting to rip off the cashier's hand banknotes. Oddly the cashier tries retreat her hand from crow's jaw; but the bird is swaying with its wing so as to scare off this teller the crow croaks: 'Kar!'—The teller alongside coworkers is freezing and dazed; and on a critical point she is letting go of the cash with a stare. By such chaos the magpie grabs fast a bundle of cash off her hand is employed its sharp beak. Next the bird sways with its wing, seen as the magpie is flying for the exit. On a whim Rob moves aside, around to exit. The crow is pronto airborne via the sliding doors that open, the bird has flown away, while seized the cash in its mouth.

The clients are waiting eager temporarily for their turn in a queue. Aside from mix-up tense, they are trying to get closer to glass-sill, whereas the others prevent them. On the spot be rowdy, and goes out of hand. Seen as a fat male grabs men's hands, whilst those women argue amid them. Next one client argues: 'It is not your turn?'—As the second customer snaps: 'We stand in a queue long time . . .'—Next the third client takes action: 'So is us! And, so did the other customers?'—Given it's become chaotic in that Bank.

In time the Bank manager is emerged, and talks using a microphone: 'Ladies and Gentlemen! Our Bank management and I regret of the situation that's arisen! Now, we ask you are all to leave the Bank! Please, come at the front . . .'—

Rosalyn and Rob second last in the queue; when she gave a secret message, ensuing of guidance to Rob: 'Son, I have doubts about this dealing process? Let us go out!'—Rob nods his head is like-minded.

Ten minutes later Rob is walking beside Rosalyn, when she deals with him. She is also seemingly edgy, while discussing: 'Son, I am desperate, what we need to do next, to pay off our debts?'-

Just as Robert and his mom have turned in a Narrow Avenue . . .

From nowhere a crow is airborne, when began swaying with its wing, and it cries out: 'Kar!'—This is a Magpie that threw a wrap beneath their feet in close proximity to those two this is good. Glance a bundle lies down on the trashes. At this instant a crow is flown away; and Rob bends down to pick it up. But

Rosalyn is afraid: 'Robert, don't pick that up!'—The teen shakes his upper arms: 'And why not, mom?—Hot on the heel, she spins to look around; seems she is worried, as she gave the impression of being nervy:—Son, what if someone, or police sees us?'—As Rob spins to look through; signs with his eyes at pack, he confirms: 'Mom, look! No one is around, only a little boy far aside!'—Next Rob is squatted on heels, as his hand is hidden that wrap, and he prolongs: 'Mom, you know we need money to pay off debts? We didn't steal that amount of cash from the bank, we are not thieves?'—She ducks her head is like-minded to Rob. Given the only witness is a kid on swing that rocks up and down.

CHAPTER 9

All but another year passes. It's a beautiful mid-summer night. Rob is now seventeen, seen him in school's hall. He is seated beside Rosalyn, Sarah-Jane and Stepfather, Hugo, also on a sit near is Margie. That Lipinski clan is rejoicing for those graduates on the Prom. Views each amid those guests are dressed in finer attires for that unique event.

Later music starts playing; and those young adults are dancing swirling in a slow waltzing across ballroom. Tag on those youths and guests, with close friends, accompanied by their parents gather . . .

The next day in dinning room is sitting around the table Rosalyn, Sarah-Jane; and her Stepfather, Hugo with Margie counts that consuming late brunch.

Afterward the door gets open, and Rob appears in doorway. Just now the whole family is taken aback. As Rosalyn's focus on her son, and in a silly says:

'Son, we thought that you would sleep much longer after the Prom?'—Rob's upper-body is in motion: 'I am not an idiot to get dead drunk? Afterward, to have hangover, and be intoxicated more? Nope!'—Rosalyn is broken up; gave a smile, saying being caring: 'Robert, we all happy that you have finished High School! Congrats!'—Next she spins to look at her husband: 'Now, Hugo and I have talked about your future, and the suitable plans of yours to chase?'—Rob ducks his head when leans, he is tempted to know: 'Mom and you're Hugo are you really think that I will make a career in the construction?'—In a flash Hugo budges in, as be certain: 'Why not! I am utterly confident that you can do it all the way, Robert! I had taught you myself, a lot! By and large you will be a great carpenter, son!'—Hearing this, Rob beams, and Rosalyn is overmuch blissful. In a short unspoken accord by all Hugo says more as is positive, and resolute: 'Okay? Rob you're young, and may well achieve anything you will put your mind to it! Working and like this studying so as to get a College degree!'—Sarah-Jane then has intruded: 'Really? Uncle Hugo, it's likely to 'happen for Rob?'—When Hugo turns aside to face her, and starts to pat the girl's hair: 'Of course it is, Sarah-Jane!'-

Just as they are joyful, Rob's interest has gone as he drops his head, is looking down into the floor.

When he gives the lowdown, yet is saddened: 'Yeah!

'My dad came yesterday to graduation; but has stayed only for a bit. He then has gone in hurry!'—Rosalyn prevents him from saying, when is incensed: 'Cause of the bitch, Tatiana! She would not let him go to see his children? Even just for a little bit?'—Rob raises his head to face her, as if he is in disbelief. He stares at Hugo, and shifts his gaze to Margie. Next Rob looks at his sister, it seems she is made a slipup: 'Mom is that true?'—Now Hugo intrudes that has made all shut up, and is involved, when tensely say-so: 'Whoa! Rob I won't be fighting for affection between Peter and you're? The truth is we are a family now, this includes me too in! But it pains me to see how you're disrespecting all of us? You're walking like a madman, being rude to Rosy and me, nearly all the time?'—Hugo takes a deep breaths; but he is stopped by Rob that bows head down, be apologetic: 'I am so sorry mom, and you too Hugo! I am not angry with you, I am mad at my dad! He's given promises, but never kept his word! Like that gory 'beach in Mexico!'—Hugo inhales; and bobs his head down: 'Okeydokey! From tomorrow on start of school holidays! I will be free from duties! Why shouldn't we go off to Miami?'-, Rob curves his head to the left; next he says-so: 'Yea! I was hoping go with my dad?'—Hugo lifts hands up, as he is joyful: 'Forget about what Peter has said? I can promise you that we will be leaving for Miami, and there relax on the Beach!'—Hugo looks around the room for support from one and all, is eager. He then is carrying on: 'Let's start packing, as will we be getting ready for a trip?'-

PART II

CHAPTER 10

In Miami is a lovely amethyst twilight. In the hotel is a suite like penthouse that located near Miami Beach. The same night in the suite is seen a pair: a woman in her late twenties, and her partner a man in his mid-forties; view as they are sitting on a couch, and watching television programs.

Eventually this couple has got bored; when the woman is involving they're leisurely, when she decided: 'I am bored sitting here! What about you?'—The man gets up of a lounge: 'So am I! Let's go to get gulps of fresh air, and swimming too?'-

Briefly the couple has dressed up; and is leaving their hotel-suite. Prior to close the door, the man looks round to make sure all of their pricey is in place. He then switched off the light: seen this pair is situated on top floor. Except they are having forgotten to close the window; after both are stepping over the threshold.

Now can be observed Miami streets up in the sky are with a nuance of Amethyst, and Stars sparking over. Outwardly view a nightfall that covered every part of ether, embracing with brilliant, like this is shown the way for tourists, who may have gone lost . . .

. . . From nowhere a bold magpie is aerial; then it descends near this hotel-suite window. The magpie at once, flew into that suite; then turns its tiny head with green eyes to view around the spacious room. Hears as the crow cries out: 'Kar!'—It fairly puts off this bird as snooped cagey, if no one is there. The magpie soars, then lands down on the surface of chest of drawers to be located rearward from a window; and grabs with its paws. The bird uses its beak so as to open a jewelry box, where this pair, which just has left, kept their gems. The magpie is poked round; and it picks up one-by-one sparked gemstones. Next the magpie places gems down on the shelf's surface. Gale has found a pendant that contained by layers of gems inside. Seen the magpie sizes two jewels in its jaws. After the bird is soaring, then passing through the open window, it has flown away . . .

. . . Sooner or later the bird returns few times in that suite. In the course of this same method the bird does it over again to pick up stuff. So far Gale has flown back-and-forth on much time, which it picked up bracelets, rings with ranges of jewelry . . .

Until the magpie began perceiving sound that someone is opening the door from outside. Hot on the hills the bird sways with its wings; and goes up in the air be wild by nature. A magpie flies away then via the open window, who knows where too?

Air travel from abodes to surroundings, has taken Gale not long, since it's to be sited not far from where the magpie is aimed for . . .

A bit later the bird lands on a tree in the midst of wide branches, where it is faded away in. In there the magpie is released part of a set, which has brought one at a time; and it thrown swiftly in a heap, where already that pile develops into a quantity. Atop of tree's branch, in a bird nest saw jewels, which's contained of gold gain with spare gems that made loads be arranged by hoard . . .

Now it's an eye-catching sunrise in Miami, with a minor wind that makes the trees shiver. At a meadow and flowers in the parks are in bud. Climate by indication of zero has aimed that supposed to be rainstorm soon outwardly. Here the view falls across chic houses, whereas the unfamiliar folks are shouting; in one a woman yells: 'Help! Thieves have stolen my valuables! Call the police, John!'-

Those residences see over in one of fancy hotels of the Community hunky-dory, where be heard mostly women voices screaming, or howling: 'Help! It was a theft! Burglars have got in the house, and stolen my jewelry! Mick, call the police! Don't you dare look around? Mick, act upon it, quickly!'-

Turn around: on other side of the town, in a hotel seen those crowds of patrons are waiting next door to this inn, whereas Rob and his family are staying in Miami on holidays. Likewise in this hotel recently was a force of entry. Hence the police forces have just arrived to investigate it. Saw few amid the forces have stopped to find out from those strangers, what they knew about the burglary.

View near that hotel as the police go in, is passing through the sliding doors.

Meanwhile, those crowds stood aside, in the hotel lobby. These rests of forces are shown up at reception desk, where having secretly investigated those, who held liable for the patrons, staying in. Hearing a man's voice from the management speaking in microphone at the reception desk, and tackling all that are turnout: 'Ladies and Gentlemen! Who are not guests in our hotel? Please, leave the 'lobby, at once!'—The patrons are formed circles, exhaled nosily story of robbery, each telling their version to the detective query. Here those employees stood aside, whereas are snooping round. Seen from one of elevators came down the couple, who were robbed on day before in the hotel? A detective nods his head; then writes notes: 'So, who do you think, raided had and stolen from you? Did you see anyone, who might be suspicious to you? One of that staffs is shaken his head from shock: 'Not really! Detective, the hotel is very respected in Miami! No one of the strangers could come without be seen by our staff first!'—They have joined that bunch of victims' off robbery; seen the first victim cries in anger, as she looks around: 'Oh, yeah? This hotel is unreliable! How burgles were ensued? You've said respectful? I vary hotel oblige to be reimbursed for my stolen jewels!'—Though the others ran back and forth in turmoil, as everyone look tense, but be in a state of chaos . . .

By the site of Miami Beach has seen those folks are having lain under the sun, while some others swam in the warm sea. Up on shore these youths and adults are playing beach volleyball. The sky hides with scree of sapphires. Not far other folks are making photographs for their future to reminisce . . .

Gaps separate the harbor: here came into the view a few young gorgeous women are walking, who wearing on bikinis that perform to do defile as their figures to be compared to the Goddesses. The womanly probably are working as Models, and have come here for a photo shot. Passing by are three young men that well built like Gods, who are pacing; then they spun around to look at womanly. Though those guys wore tops and shorts, but being spotted damp through their clothes, and they are paying attention to the models. Spur of the moment hearing one of those men are in sweet-talking to the women: 'Hey, gorgeous! Water is

warm! I am inviting you are to go for a swim?'—The second guy
stops him, when single-handle props up: 'Yeah, girls! He is right!
Come on, let us all go for a swim?'—But one of the girls' snaps:
'Listen, dudes! Were you going before somewhere?'—The second
male points a hand uphill: 'Yeah! We are! Now, we are curious, if
'you have stopped over there, in that fancy hotel, by a chance?'—
This other girl reacts, be cynical: 'What if we are? It's like Angela
told you before, why don't you walk, keep straight, far-off, and
then you split?'—Then again the first guy reacts: 'Girls you are
hostile, for that reason all of you are needed to bite your tongues!'-

In next to no time those men are walking away from unfriendly
models.

While Rob stood aside, and has heard their quarrel.

Later that day stopping at Miami Beach is Rosalyn, Sarah-
Jane beside Hugo that came up to Rob at the same time is holding
useful photos. This proves that one and all seem is in high spirits.
Now Rosalyn and Hugo's eyes screw up; just then those are laid
hands up over their eyes too browse, with the purpose of hiding
from high sun-ray of such effect. Next Hugo alone tackles all the
Lipinski, is amused: 'Don't you think that Climate is beautiful

in Miami?'—All in chorus rejoined with joy: 'Yes! Climate here is amazing!'—Hugo is thrilled: 'Rosy! I feel like to fly away! As I have plans for us! Family, are we having a good time or what?'— All in unison jiggle their heads in harmony: 'It's utterly fab to swim?'—Hugo gave to all a hint: 'We can get hungry, and have a bite later! Let us go for a swim, as one? How is that for a start? 'Family, don't you agree?'—They glance apiece, and are sharing his delight. Next views, as they all are moving toward the warm Sea for a swim.

Some time pass since Lipinski have stayed on the beach. Rob has surfaced from the sea, spotted salty stays resting on his skin texture, while it is soaking. Rosalyn offers her son a towel; then signs with her hand to side road; says be jolly: 'Son, Hugo and I must go someplace. Can you take Sarah to a Café on the other side for ice-cream? You will enjoy too!'—Rob smiles, and nods: 'No problem, mama! Just give us some cash for it, will you?'-

A bit later Rob and Sarah-Jane are walking in the café, where they have taken seats in. Concurrently those two are glanced around with interest. Briefly a waiter comes up to whereas Rob and Sarah are sitting, and offers the bill of fares, then he is asking them: 'What would like to order?'—Rob slants head down, and reads the menu: 'We want to order two ice-creams with chocolate tops, please!'—Waiter is in fine manners: 'Of course! Do you want liqueur to be served on top with your sweets?'-

Robert and Sarah-Jane haven't even finished eating ice-cream. Unpredicted blue vanished from the sky, where instead a giant grey cloud being covering sky up and afar, which it filled the air?

Up-to-the-minute a thunderous clap is heard at the open-air, followed by that hear ever more. Is drawn to one time, where spotting the Miami streets were overflowing with rainwater. Sun-rays evaporate from the sky; on the spot those folks in the streets are hiding in all places, where they can possible find it on their way, or cover up them with things.

Whilst in the café milieu Rob and Sarah-Jane looked at each other: given they have worn minor clothes that both hesitant. On a whim Sarah-Jane drawbacks is protesting with hand gestures to her brother, and too is fussy: 'Rob, what we are going to do? How can we walk to our hotel?'—Now Rob is amused: 'Do you see a rainstorm for the first time? Are you a sugar baby to be melted? Look, we have plastic bags here to hide our heads over with?'—She thinks for a bit; then puts a smile, and decides: 'It's true, Rob! We will be running?'- Rob is returning: 'Yes!'- Now, she is happy: 'Let's go, then?'-

A bit later see Rob accompanied by Sarah-Jane left the café; and both are walking along boulevard, where plenty of trees to be spotted. Yet the rain lessens.

A sister and brother start crossing the road, route which they are chosen to be avoiding pools of water across by their paces.

Unforeseen a crow is airborne, whilst Rob and his sister just turned around the corner. The crow flew, and has stained Sarah-Jane's blouse on her upper body, by way of poop be spotted, so the girl proves by; she jumps aside, and bows her head to prove it:—What is that? A bird did that? I think it was a crow flew by? Yes! Obviously, look Rob a crow flew and has leaked poop on my T-shirt!—Rob appears be lost in thoughts; next he's stated, yet is dreamy: 'Listen, I will get you to our hotel! But I must go someplace, okay sis? . . .'—

By hotel's entry Rob stood close to Sarah-Jane. Being an elder brother, Robert gives his younger sister precept, though he is telling her firmly: 'Oh, come on, Jane! Don't make a scene? If mom with Hugo do come back, and ask for me? Just tell them I won't be long! All right, sister?'—But Sarah seems is prying on her brother, when sees if she gets out of him in sweet talks:—Where are you going, Robby? Miami is a strange place. But you don't have friends here! I am sure of that!'—Here Rob's face alters; he bows his head. Given that her tongue is in cheek: 'Or maybe you have met a girl? Come on brother, tell me all about it?'—It's sunk to Rob, so he is gloomy; and in a firm says: 'Shut up, Sarah! I told you I have to go! That what it is! As for you, Jane, stop asking stupid question! It's not civil! Now, go in the room and wait for mom and Hugo's arrival! But if they are not coming soon? Wait for them in the foyer then, Sarah!'-

In time Rob is walking along Miami streets.

Later he turns around the corner, whereas on the way, he has bought some meals . . .—

By now evening has come. Rob walks toward the plaza; at distant saw the crow is soaring; and on the spot he's identified it is a magpie. Saw outside is still raining, Robert following on pace, where the crow glided to. Predominantly everyone has vanished from the streets by heavy rain.

So far, Robert is pursuing magpie Gale that being airborne. Spur of the moment, he is probing: 'Gale, will you show me the way? But why, and where to?'-

Soon he's approached secluded; where high on a tree saw the magpie that is flown in a flash with wrapped stuffs in its beak. Seen as Gale is landing on top of a wide branch, where nests have been set.

What the input in core if trees that is shown up trunks, which have contained of brushwood. Whatever thing has hidden in for a human be unimaginable; view that area be in the best position. A magpie act like is alluring Rob to climb the tree, where it is traced in a bird nest. The crow's cry, as its echo is heard. Rob extends a hand, be dull: 'Gale, why the hell I have to climb up the tree?'—. . . Though Rob is trying to climb the tree, but he's grumpy; ahead of his attempt has searched round the area, to be sure no-one passed by.

The magpie first lands on a tree with wide branches, where is resting on primitive nest. Odds—on it layers being made of twigs, or after these Birds were picking up shrubs and grass in anywhere.

After Rob climbs up the tree, he is squatting near a bird nest. At the bottom of nest where the bird are supposed to lay down an egg? Instead Rob's eyes fixed on rise from a lot of gold by ranges of jewelry. It sinks to him at once: all amazes Rob; here he says in a shaky voice: The jewels are identical, which were stolen from the hotel, where we stay or elsewhere, which knew?'—Rob is re-leaved ineptly, as being in a state of shock: 'Did you steal these jewels, Gale?'—A crow comeback with: 'Kar!'—He ducks: 'Spot-on!'— But Rob senses he has got himself in hot waters: 'What if I take jewels with me to the hotel, randomly the Cops pop in and search our rooms? God forbid, we end up in jail, on theft?'—At this point Rob's hushed; he then angles his head towards the bird, and is affirmed: 'How did you accomplished it, Gale? What can I tell my folks on the stuffs, be from? What 'should I do with the gems?'— Still he stays be amazed, and remained so, for some time . . .

Transiently saw the rain is sagging as it gave a sign to Robert sliding down from that tree of fortune. This teenager keeps staring on jewelry, so far he is spellbound, without a hint that being drawn in and possessed by the enhancements. So as to save it Rob takes off his T-shirt, then splits gold from gems, and wraps up that stuff into two heaps separate. He wraps half of each evenly; next enfolds stuff in his shirt, and covers it. Rob packs stuff in a plastic bag, just to ensure these don't get soaked. Despite his temptation,

Rob is afraid to carry jewelry in the hotel without being exposed, and not to endanger his family. He bows head down, and talks to himself: 'I must think clear, and be careful, consider how too act? Okay, Gale, I have to go! I will think of something . . .'—

The next day, at dusk, Rob is observing; then is rushing in secluded area, close to the park. Except he has forgotten: 'Where is that tree with magpie's jewels be located?'— A sudden idea came in his mind: to call magpie in verse . . .

. . . Rob is unable to finish the rhymes, when seen the magpie airborne wildly above him, and being swaying with its wing; then heard the crow cries out.

Views the bird lands over on the wide tree's branches. Rob tackles magpie at once, like the bird grasps human saying; as he appears is amazed: 'Hi, Gale! So, will you show me the way to the tree where that precious nest of yours is?'—A crow croaks:— Kar!-, Rob puts a smile; shakes his shoulders, and stares with a stun:—Gosh, you're very clever bird? Do you know, what people would say?'—Timbre of a crow's cry is heard: 'Kar!'—Rob smiles; and ducks his head: 'Okay, then! Show me the way! And, Gale I brought food of your choice!'-

CHAPTER 11

The next day in a condo to be heard the phone rang! Peter in there gets of the couch; is on foot, as responding: 'Hello! Peter, speaking?'—Robert in hotel-room is listening tensely; next he retorts, as is panting on the telephone: 'Dad, I am glad you 'have picked up the phone? I need your help! Can you fly to Miami, today?'—On other side of the phone line Peter listens with languor, what his son is saying; he then alone replies: 'Rob, is it you? What is going on? Listen, why you are in Miami?'-

Inn Rob listens attentively; he then talks in desperate voice: 'All of us are in Miami! Dad, when you land, I will explain to you all about . . .'—Peter's forlorn, when listens; and he also looks through a window: 'Son, tomorrow Tatiana and I need to fly back home . . .'—Rob listens impatiently. But he disrupts him by saying: 'Now, I realize that dad! But I urgently need to see you! Can you at least once in your life help me?'—Peter's voice is edgy: 'Son we will lose our air tickets? We have stayed there long enough . . .'—Rob listens wary, when all at once stops him, and came back in a tense voice: 'Listen dad, if my stuff has not been urgent I would not bother you! Your trip to Miami will be utterly on business! Trust me, dad please, delay your flight, better come to Miami?'—Now Peter listens wary; when he reacts with a query:' Okay, let's say I am coming! What about your mom and 'Hugo, if they see me, what will they think? Don't they know how to help you out? No matter what it is? Tell me, son!'—Robert's voice in hoarseness: 'No! I cannot tell you over the phone; its setback, of what has ensued? But I won't go to jail! Trust me, that is a potential profit in it for your, dad! The main thing I will tell you when you get here!'—They are breathing; while both thinking. In a critical point Peter inhales; and breaks silence is declaring: 'I'm sorry, son! I'm not going to come . . .'

Robert became sad, thus he's terminated the call.

At the same evening Hugo and Rosalyn entered the lobby, and are walking right to the reception desk. A sudden telephone began buzzing: Ring! And, one of that hotel staff answers the call, hears is saying.

Another member of management leans up front, while murmurs to Hugo:—Good evening, sir!—In his turn, Hugo asks politely: 'Good evening! Do you have any messages for the Lipinski family?'—Sees one more from that staff moves up and down the stairs. As one of the management tells Hugo: 'As a matter of fact we do! Can I speak to you in private, sir?'-

Hugo nods his head; then turns to face Rosalyn, and puts a smile. He points to her go upon taken lift; he then turns back to this staff member: 'Yes! Who is the massage from?'—This man from staff leans over the counter; and handles to Hugo a piece of paper, which he view, it's to be folded up. Given that Hugo reads it. After his face has turned pale.

Later that night, Robert comes up to Waterfront; views he is under your own steam.

He has advanced; rushing across the road to the Café, which is located on Miami's Seaside.

When Rob came within an inch of café, from gap saw his Stepfather, Hugo is seated at table that, seeming being dull. Hugo

too is glance at Rob; when he waves his arms up in the air . . .
Once Rob is drawn near Hugo's sit, and without losing a second
he gets down to business, with Stepfather. On a whim Hugo stops
him, and alone speaks bluntly: 'Rob, I don't see why you have
left me a note, and asked to come in secret to this Café? Instead,
you're playing games with me!'—Now Robert looks around, he
then tells: 'Listen Hugo, if my problem wasn't 'urgent, I wouldn't
bother you . . .'—Rob on the spot breathes in; but looks lost;
and he prolongs:—First of all before I could tell you a great deal
of secret, promise that you will help me, Hugo?—Now, both
are looking into each-other's eyes. Hugo in his turn suspects
the worst; resultant he shakes with his upper arms, be edgy:—
Robert, what is so urgent that you drag me here? Can't your
father or Rosy chip in the situation?'—The teen is gloomy, and
begun talking:—I called my dad, but he didn't care to help me!
Do you think he gave a toss? I won't tell mom either about its
too risky?'—He leans toward Hugo; and whispers:—No! You're
wrong, Hugo! I guess you the only one I can trust! So, I didn't
drag you for nothing!'—Robert bows his head down; and in
one go, places a hand in his pocket. He removes plastic bag, in
which it is packed; he then unties fabric; impends to view a heap

that Rob has put up on the table. See these jewels are totally unpacked: 'That's why I have begged you to come here! Now you know. Have you ever seen is as amazing as this, Hugo?'—Once Hugo sees these jewels have become nervous; he grabs heap out off table; and gets down so as to hide it underneath. Be shaken, his reaction with stunning look; but by a stern whispers: 'Rob, are you out of your mind? What if anyone saw you? We will be fallen in deep shit! Where in hell did you get that stuff? Did you steal those jewels from?'—Rob stops him, in a gloomy voice reacts: 'In fact, I didn't! I am not a thief! I have found jewelry in a bird's nest upon the tree . . .'—Hugo disrupts Rob with a look around of suspicion; and saw to it by a whisper: 'Son, I was not born yesterday? Or if you think I am stupid? Since jewelry don't lie in nests just like this, or grow on trees, son?'—But Rob stops him, be snobby: 'I haven't said jewels growing on trees? Though Hugo, don't you want listen to my reasons?'—Those two are looking at each-other without a sound. Just then Rob is clued-up: 'Hugo, you know that day before yesterday was raining?'—Hugo ducks his head. On a critical point Rob reveals more: 'I was hiding from the rain in plaza. Sudden a crow flew, and has held a tiny bag in its beak. So, I have gone after the bird, and climbed the tree! There

I have found jewels in a nest . . .'—Rob stops; breathes, and is continuing with his story: 'Now, I wouldn't have a clue, what to do with that stuff?'—Rob looks forlorn, as is panting intensely. For that reason he looks in Hugo's eyes with a plead: 'Will you help me seal the deal with jewels or not, man?'—Hugo shakes his head in a merger, and looks is backing him up; whispering: 'Okay, son! I will get in touch with a big shot. You and I are staying put, but the family must leave right away!'-

CHAPTER 12

It seems divine fall; tree-leaves have gained rose-brown nuance. At that season's climate be seen of many wet days; but shrubs have dried up from the frost, are lying around shores. Today is a wintry night, which doesn't predict to be rainy coming . . .

Anyplace far in a high-rise building came into view a woman in her apartment, is having a shower. In an apartment the water is flickering, as it's running; whereas can be observed a window is ajar open.

From nowhere a magpie soars near, as is aimed for the apartments block window. Once Gale has seen that no one around; the bird is flown in. Already inner the magpie is soaring over twice, and lands down into surface on the chest of drawers. There in can be observed a jewelry-box, where woman-owner has kept in accessories. Now Gale is worn a mini bag that, hang down from its neck. The magpie opens box is using its beak, and starts pecking jewels. Next the bird captures one precious stone, when employs its jaws that, is kept in tough. Then the magpie throws gems one-by-one into a tiny bag to be made out of aluminum. After the mission has ended, Gale in a full swing is swaying by its wings, before taken to the air. Next the crow flies through an open window; and is on its way toward . . .

At outer walls, prior to fly away, the magpie hums with liking it: 'Kar-Kar-Kar!'-

The crow is aerial extensively; as by its next turn the bird goes left, like so is changed the fly course. Soon the magpie descends, close to Robert's house, with its aim of landing . . .

CHAPTER 13

Here is a violet sunrise by inception? As in one residence appeared Martin, who is into a deep sleep in his boudoir? . . .

Miraculously his bedroom door gets open, and on the entry appears a stranger. This visitor smirks on the spot; given he senses that Martin stinks with alcohol, which he drank in a bar, on day before; in the company of some other dudes . . .

Next the visitor came near Martin's bed, in a flash began talking to Martin in a brogue, presumably he is French: 'I guess your name is Martin?'—Martin couldn't believe his eyes, as he slowly gets of his bed, still is stunned. Seen his head slants to the right, and he murmurs: 'Yes it is! Who are you, sir? What are you doing in my room?'—The man is nosy: 'I think you had read a book titled "Le Miserable"?'—Assumed teen is amazed: 'Oh yea, sir!

'"Le Miserable" all the time my favored book!'-

. . . Definition by Javert was of 'Le Miserable', the inspector being respecting the Law above all. Javert resolutely has chased an escaped convict, Valijean, been hoping bring him to justice.

The man's image says firm; but slowly: 'Now, young man 'I know that you have an enemy, and who made hard for you to get accepted in the Academy? Being caused, when you were harmed: 'So, I praise you to do something about this Rob. Pay him back!'—

Mysteriously the French detective is vanished, just as he has shown up. When Martin looks around for Javert, but this man is nowhere to be found. This teen rubs his eyes, and shakes with upper body; given that it was figment of his sick imagination. On spur-of-the-moment Martin reminiscent what Hugo has divulged to him for Rob's apprentice job as a Builder? Martin begun recalling what Hugo has divulged to him and Jonah yesterday, in Downtown at the Bar; but he is impulsive.

At night back then, whereas Martin be seated alongside Jonah and a few more mates. They were drinking liquor, where hearing music being played. Foolishly Martin yells, as be content: 'Guys, let's have another drink?'—Apiece nod their head, and looking around; while they are waiting for more shots of Whisky from the bartender to be served . . .

Moments later, suddenly at the entry have emerged two men, one of whom is Morales, Martin's ex-teacher that is walking in the bar beside a stranger. Next those two have approached a counter; and taken sits a length away from a gang, which is drinking there. Now Martin is 'like a cat on a hot tin roof', as spanks over Hugo's shoulder: 'Mister Morales, evening?'—Of silly shock Hugo turns to glance at a person, be tense: 'Good evening to you too, Martin!—Hugo is spotting Jonah and these rest of familiar faces:—I see, you're not alone here, Martin?—Martin smirks; and nods his head: 'Yeah. Why are you here, sir?'—Hugo turns around; gave a signal to a stranger that is seated at the counter; as he gave the impression of being displeased; as he browse up: 'A man is my good mate, we used to work together. We came to get a drink, like was in the past since he's a true friend?'—Hugo winks to his guest, and is slapped over the man's upper-body.

A sudden Jonah comes up to join that party, and slaps him, so as to make his presence known. Now Hugo talks candidly to them: 'Have the two of you considered getting a job?'—Martin seems is lost; he has taken breaths; his shoulders are shaky: 'I have no idea of Jonah's plans? Though, I 'didn't think about myself, yet?'—Hugo shakes his upper-body: 'That's why I am here with my friend! I want Rob to get a job in the constructions . . .'—

Plus Martin recalls what Javert has said; so he turns be angry: 'You dickhead, Lipinski! I accuse you for my failure to not getting in the Academy! My life is rotten and useless, inspector was right? I will help him, not! Rob, you will be gasping the last breath!'-

Presently it's seen a sapphire crack of dawn. Atop on the construction site, seen those two men are erecting on and having employed dozens of Scaffolds. At the precinct is resting some spare equipment, whereas safety harnesses have been installed earlier.

Given that one amid those riggers are unpacking working tools. Apparently this man is in mid-thirties, and his name happen is Billy Gallagher. He is a typical looking man; fair-haired, blue-eyed; and medium-to-tall of his height. Billy looks down from altitude at one casement, which has not been equipped yet; hence he expresses laughter. Despite job is uncompleted, by and large structure shown far above the ground: as a crow's fly. Above the building side concrete has been set up, like brushwood is fixed posts, upfront to be viewed foundations, in which adjoined with set of high-rises. Up on the roof far-sighted a crowd of that workforce amid those is young Lipinski. Back then Hugo, Robert's stepfather arranged a career for his Stepson; and had got him into constructions. Just as Rob has got accepted in apprentices that aimed for him new trade; and have prepared to develop into the joiner's job.

Whilst down on the ground observes around these builds is the boss Merrimack. Given he is going up on the elevator. Visible as the boss has approached that working team, amidst whom Robert is sighted too nearby . . .

In a while, during the break time Rob is approached by Merrimack who addresses him; but this teen being candid: 'Mister Merrimack, I talked to Billy and he has promised take me under his wings! So can I join side for trainees so as to become a rigger?'—But he is interrupted by Merrimack, who says-so is worried: 'Look, Rob you're a nice young man, but 'untrained! My advice to you is don't put yourself through stupid risks?'—As Rob debates: 'Mister Merrimack, I love be on peak, and become a skilled rigger! Like it's full of adrenalin in me!'—Merrimack is shaking his head, but looks genuinely concerned: 'Rob, listen to me, son if God forbids anything happens to you? Your parents will never forgive me for that! Hugo, specially!'—Rob is energized: 'Can I at least try to do it? If not, I will go back to be a trainee for the joiner's job!'—Merrimack looks at this teenager with a smile; he then says-so, but being gloomy: 'When I talked to your Step-father, we both have agreed for you to become a joiner? And, yet . . .'—

CHAPTER 14

Present its hours of darkness, herein at the construction site a person be spotted, worn on camouflage. Seen as step-by-step, a stranger is shifting toward lifts. Given that buildings are carrying on rosters there. In spite of projects have not been residential yet, but established builds almost be ready for the inspections. Now a man's image talks in an accent: 'Don't disappoint me, Martin, you have to prove to be Heroic, by execute it!'—Be heard as an odder talk to himself: 'Okay, I know what to do!'-

The visitor enters premises, where those workforces have held their operating tools. In due course those would remove cables that does fit in the riggers job, which have used it for. A stranger has worn black glove, as his head be covered with balaclava. He then comes near a metal box, indicates to one and opens it, where saw a tag named 'Robert Lipinski'. When the visitor puts a hand in his pocket, and inserts from a bulky army knife. He is resultant and begun cutting off in-a-half rigger's cords. Briefly the visitor places ropes back into the drawer; he then locks up access. After before exiting, he has made sure no one saw him, so, he looks around. Next, like a Ghost this visitor, is begun walking off the site.

At sunrise on this construction side in the course of working saw the Safety harnesses' and ropes have been installed, whereas placed in the middle of the erected structures, by those riggers.

The same morning Rob arrives at work is felt good, and immediately undertaken by team of riggers; sees him being in good mood. On premises are spotting those workers' changed into cladding aimed for a construction job. Next Rob opens the box's drawer, and removes from a set of ropes and shackles, which those riggers would have employed for their safety. Given safety harnesses, amid one of that is doyen the rigger's rope. At this time is spotting that crew of riggers with team leader, Billy Gallagher. Billy, who is nosy, on the spot has a chat with Rob: 'What is your name, lad?'—Robert is nervy, as reacting gently: 'Rob! I mean,

Robert Lipinski!'—Billy puts a smile; then allows advice to Rob: 'Listen dude, you're starting today as a trainee. 'You amateur for that reason, I want to give you helpful hint try hard lad, but don't overdo it? 'Cause my team and I have qualified for that sort of a job!'—Rob seems is overjoyed, his eyes with a glow that, he makes sense: 'Okay. Can I call you Billy?'—Billy nods his head, at the same time he laughs, is like-minded. Yet Robert is enduring: 'Billy, if you only know how much I love extreme jobs? When I am atop, it feels as if takes my breath away! And butterflies alike are tickling in my stomach!'—Billy stops him, when gives a shake with his upper arms; he then takes off gloves: 'You strike for me a chord of youths, who are seeking extreme mixed with adrenalin! Rob, you're something else?'—Billy looks at him; gave a wink; and points to ropes that lie down nearby: 'Let us swap the ropes? I give you my and you pass me yours? Ahead to get with the job, fix cable cords proper up on yourself, lad!'—Here Rob gladly swaps ropes with him: 'Okay, I will do it boss!'-, Rob acts in response. Billy spins round, and tells that entire team: 'Let us all descend! Rob, you're held on tight, as you slide down? Don't look down, or else 'your head can start to spin! Lad, look straight, never down, and be on alert!'—Rob is ecstatic: 'Okay, Billy! Thanks a lot, boss!

I am ready, when you are!'—Billy looks round as tackles that team with Robert counted: Okay! There in, we go! Let us jump down, dudes!'—Next the riggers jump from altitude: on elevated extreme over the tops of edifice, and pass via build by these teams of least five that are hanged down. Like so they are having held balance up in the air. Since the teams have clung safely to cable cords, then slowly but surely them been in motion. Those riggers intend is bungee jumping; once them landing down on their two legs, which by they're next drive having made on balcony. This team has jumped: Jump! But Rob is an amateur that seems being disoriented. To scrutiny those riggers are sliding down smoothly. Impulsively, Rob yells: 'Whoa! It takes my breath away! I am flying! Can you hear me, Billy?'—That team with Robert is counted, began jumping down to a few yards more . . .

A sudden rope under Billy's body began tearing apart. Given that Rob has hanged above him. Though Billy doesn't know yet of the broken rope. So, Rob's breath is caught in, as he saw danger and freezes without a fig how to reacting in a difficult situation? Seen Rob's eyes wide open of fear, given Billy slips down of a tad that, gave a warning by yelling: 'Billy! Look out for your ropes!'— But Billy can't hear him, instead is fixed his eyes across. Parallel as Billy is kept sliding down . . . Whilst low-slung, the rigger is curving sideways: unforeseen his ropes have slashed; then it's sunk to him gage what arose at this juncture . . .

Whereas, down on the ground everyone seem grown to be in a state of chaos, when workers on the spot have realized off a fear, they run back and forth. Rob is scared stiff, and tries preventing Billy from a tragic fall. In a flash the teen bravely swings, then cuts rope up of the rigger's weight that is hanged askew, as ready to split, while he's stable. Billy is in close proximity, and ready to step in. Then Rob yells on top of his lungs: 'Billy! Hold on tight! I will try rolling you up to upper level!'-Billy is sped and dropping; then crashes down on a blocked wall with his head. As a result Billy of it loses consciousness.

CHAPTER 15

A few months pass. It's the end of Easter. Across-the-board is spring: whilst the plants are blooming. From a place near is heard music on the open-air, Rob walking along the streets, as is deep into his thoughts? Once he draws near musician's band, a sudden yells being heard amid those that be meant for Rob. There saw Martin, who briskly folds a hand like it's a gun; and is talking by scorn: 'Hey, you're, criminal! I hope you get a fair sentence?'-

Hearing this Rob's head falls into his shoulders, and is edgy. He starts running away at once. As the gang is repeated singing that, be heard across . . .

In due course of actions, this has caused Robert for be convicted. Thus, he ends up in the Court of Law. View in the courtroom the Judge is a woman, in her late forties that, ruled here; when she speaks in a clear, but firm voice: ' . . . Be caused by industrial accident that ensued with the plaintiff, who has worked as a rigger. This resulted, when Mister Gallagher had tumbled down from an altitude; and made hard for him to go on working? Moreover, 'it has caused plaintiff been inoperative, but above all injuries!'—A Judge raises her head; then has a firm gawk, and is focused on Rob. She takes breaths; then monotony is prolonged: 'What the attorney for the plaintiff has to say, about this case?'—The attorney is returned: 'Thank you is Honor! I wish to call on witness stand Mister Gallagher the plaintiff!'—Billy is tense, but keen: 'You're an Honor! The respectful Jury! Ladies and Gentlemen! I wish to tell you about Rob!'—He does stop; then shakes his head: 'Sorry, I meant to say: the defendant is just a kid!'—He turns and points at Rob; he then says more: 'I want all in court to look at him? Does this boy know a thing about life? No! On one thing I am sure, if he was back, then up there instead of me, he wouldn't survive!'—He stops talking; looks at Rob; breathes deeply; and is pleading: 'Being a skilled rigger, even I was unable to handle that situation well! Now, I want ask members of the Jury and you're an Honor to express sympathy for 'defendant! I forgave Lipinski! It wasn't his fault! It was just a hard luck on that day?'- All in the courtroom became silent; excluding Rob, who seem being scared. Saw Rosalyn cried, as her husband Hugo be seated near.

After two hours of recess the Judge is emerged again; and began reading a verdict. Given Rob has stood up, so that he is learning of his fate. The Judge reads in clear tells: '. . . Injunction, where defendant worked at the constructions. Of what was an industrial accident that caused the plaintiff harm? This has left plaintiff be inoperative that affected Mister Gallagher, from the time he became lengthily crippled!'—The Judge looks down on papers; breathe in, and proclaims: 'Which has reveled evidence that were presented to the Court! The fact that defendant is a minor, I Bylaw, rule for Mister Lipinski to get one year of sentence! Due to Defendant being a juvenile; therefore, from now Mister Lipinski must remain on probation . . .'—At this point is befell silence. Next the Judge raises her head up; looks at Robert, and she declares . . .

CHAPTER 16

See the weather is fine at this evening with a lot of bright stars shining in the skies. Someplace far-flung a woman in high-rise-building apartment is having a shower. Hear the water is running inner. Within apartment the window is ajar, as it swings back and forth.

A sudden magpie is taken wings, and drawn near an aimed unit's window. The bird has observed around: no one there; and it flew in via a wide-open window. Soaring twice over, the bird is landing on the surface of chest of drawers. Down there comes into view be a box, where the owner has kept costume jewelry. At this time Gale has worn a mini-bag that hanged down from its tiny neck, which was made of aluminum. The magpie opens the box, is employing its beak; and began pecking jewels one by one. The magpie hoists one precious stone amidst having many, is using its beak; and kept tough inside bird's jaw. The magpie keeps on, as throws gems one-by-one in a mini-bag. Once the bird effort was achieved; it sways with wings; is underway by taken to the air; and flew through a window-glass. The bird is spotted, as it has arrived on the site.

Here, the magpie is on its way to a secluded area . . .

At the same night in secluded area, prior to flyaway, the magpie hums, as if it likes that task. A Crow's cry is heard all around: 'Kar-kar-kar!'-

Much later the bird is soaring for a time, as it's headed for a certain site. When a crow turns left; next it has changed the fly course. A minute ago the crow flew; and descends close to Rob's house, where it is landing.

CHAPTER 17

All but two years pass. Here is a beautiful summer night. Rob is by now twenty years of age.

At the moment sees in lounge room Rob's Stepfather, Hugo with the entire Lipinski family is sitting around the table, and drank tea. Given that mood between the Lipinski having felt stressed out. Whilst Hugo appears be edgy: 'Look, Rob, many of us had run of hard luck! Now you have found yourself in an similar situation?'—Hugo stops; is gasping; and tell more: 'We all need to go with the flow! If you think you're alone, and being unfortunate? What about Billy? How does he feel being crippled for a long time?'—Hugo stops of talking; has taken gulps of air; he then indicates: 'You will be okay, son, 'but remember this death is the worst punishment for all! Until we breathe, we can exist!'— All is taken a lungful of air. Rosalyn has a word to say, as shaken her head; but she is kind: 'Son, it's true! Don't be sad? Hugo and I even your dad would not leave you to be! Will you be back at work since your redundancy, if Hugo can talk to VIP?'—She seems is gloomy. But Rob stops her; as he bows head down: 'No, thanks! Mom and you're Hugo just have born a baby, he is my bro! Despite my attachment to all of you are, I wish to fly away! Like so, I have decided to flee!'—Rosalyn is distressed to cry:

'Where do you plan to go, son? Wander around the world? Will be someone taken care of you?'—Saw Rob is distressed to cry: 'Mom and you Hugo I can't take it anymore! Everyone blamed me for God knows what? I hear some folks have reproached me and accused from the time when the disaster occurred? Mom, don't worry about a thing, I will take care!'-

PART III

CHAPTER 18

As the evening began, in train's restaurant sees Rob is seated around table. On the other side of the table is a young man. Pays attention that he's of Chinese appearance. This man in his mid or late twenties; is dressed in casual, as he edgily gawks around. Rob meanwhile, observes him, and is asking: 'My name is Robert! Who are you, and where is it you from?'—This man raises his head up; and replies: 'Well, my name is Dan Ming, and I am being a proud Chinese American!'—Yet Rob is nosy: 'Are you traveling alone? Where do you live? I mean in which state you're going to?'—But Rob doesn't react.

Even if Dan is tense; by taken a deep breathe; but he seems to laid-back: 'I have visited my family in China! Now I am returning home to Pittsburgh from that trip. Oh, and Robert, what about you're?'-

A bit later, for mealtimes in front of Robert and Dan's eyes on boards are placed sets in, whereas cuisines having served up on the trays. Once Ming has taken delivery of his meals from a stewardess; seen as he began munching it without delay. Next Dan signals to Rob's at the chows: 'Why won't you eat something?'—But, Rob takes a deep breath; shakes his head as is refused: 'No, thanks. Don't see to me! Just have your own bites?'—Lastly Rob does the same, once he is ordered equal meals to . . .

Passing through the night Rob is aboard the Amtrak train that departing, whereas these schedule stops to be supposed by it. Briefly Rob stares in the windowsill, where saw a lost crow is soaring: it's turned out being his magpie. He is grown nervy, and froze in his seat.

A sudden magpie drops; then hangs in the air. Next a magpie has drawn near window that, is matching Rob's sit; and Gale gawks via glass-sill into his eyes. On a whim, he is drawn window's curtain away.

Later light off, in every part of the train is dark. Since it is night, travellers fell asleep.

At dawn, train 'Amtrak' breaks to a halt; and is arriving in Pittsburgh at 4.46 a.m. Outside the Rail Station, hear a deep biting voice from amp let know those passengers on be scheduled info to leave the train at once.

Seen the passengers from train have disembarked at last . . .

Later from the waist down amid those travelers saw Rob that is carrying a luggage. On the spot he makes a stop, turns around to observe anew place, where he has arrived in. Rob looks around with curiosity, but listens warily. A sudden he glances Dan nearby, so he is asking him: 'Do you know a place I can rent, Dan?'—Dan looks be uneasy: 'Not really. Listen, it was nice meeting you. But, I have to run! Okay?'—Rob's look as if his be lost at sea: 'Dan, wait a second! Can I at least get your phone number? Just in case? . . .'—

A bit later: Rob along with those travelers goes through sliding doors in, have entered Pittsburgh's Terminal. He then is walking unstopped upfront.

CHAPTER 19

A few months have past, from the time when Rob has moved in to Pittsburgh. The city is visited the fall season, still climate there be unkindly cold.

One upon a night Rob is walking alongside a girl, since they have met lately on the railway station. The girl's name Eleanor Lonsdale or Nora that is eighteen, going on nineteen. She has beautiful features; is slim, Nora's look being like a sporty one; with light skin texture. This pair is at their easy going, that Rob starts chitchat. He looks at her, produce a smile; but be humble: 'Eleanor, I know that we have met not so long ago? But can I call you Nora?'—Her cheeks turn pink by a nervy grin: 'Yes, you can!'—And Robert prolongs: 'I have a favor to ask of you're?'— Nora's browsed up, even if she beams: 'What is it you need?'— Rob seems is ashamed, but asks her anyway: 'You see, I arrived 'here recently. All is strange too many? No have I rights to stay in Dorm? Cause I am studying part time in College! But I awfully need a place to live in? And I'm willing to pay any price for rent! Nora, have you heard of any vacant? Can you help me to find one?'—She smiles, and nods with her head: 'It is possible for me to help you! In fact, you're in luck, Robert! My family owns a cottage a bit far-off Pittsburgh? It's desirable site, as is around thirty minutes of traveling to city centre and from our College!'— Now he alters to be keen; and states without delay: 'I can hardly believe it! Nora, are you sure your family would not mind renting bungalow to me?'—Nora is laughing; as she became pleasantly polite: 'I am positive! They are away at this point! Not many keen to rent on this time of the year since winter season is coming! Firstly, you have to see our bungalow, Robert? I hope you like it after all, with having faults in? And, we have a loft upstairs too?'—Now Robert is pleasantly amazed: 'Are you kidding me? Of course, I want to get there, and see your place? And, Nora, you call me Rob!'—Nora at once hides her joy, like so she has said nicely: 'Then bungalow is yours! If you are desperate to stay in there, Rob?'-

CHAPTER 20

Over three months pass by. It's still is late fall in the city. Now saw ways in the park; whereas Robert is walking along the path on a superb sunset, following him alongside is Dan Ming.

Later those two are walking for a fair mile. Next both make a turn in out-of-the-way, to take a break; around they are seated down on a bench. There be overheard as those two are having a chat. Dan is first asking him over: 'Rob, how your things going?'— Robert raises his head up; breathes in, but he seems is dull: 'I wish it could be better!—He reveals to Dan of life chronicle, without given away all facts about him, as be wary.

All at once, on the other side of Pittsburgh, meets Martin McDermott, who has left the building.

Moments later, McDermott is begun crossing the road; whilst he has headed for the railway station . . .

In next to no time Martin is walking through suburban. After he walks in his abode. As he looks around in the room, where it is gloomy: curtains are obscured. He stops curtly near to the table, whereas stood a bottle of Whisky. Apart from liquor saw lays a syringe that he crabs fast; it seems all is set for Martin to inject himself with drugs . . .

At the same time, back in the park Rob and Dan are taken gulp of air, and into their own thoughts. Dan's look as if his be concerned: ' . . . Rob, how you have crooked into a deep shit?'—Rob's look be gloomy, when he spoke: 'I worked in the constructions; back then it was endued of an industrial accident, ropes had got ripped off, and a worker being hurt! I have received a year of the prison terms. But a Judge overruled has changed my sentence to probation for good behavior, so you see now . . .—Ming's breathing deepens, somewhat seems sinks to him; so he shakes with his head, and says kindly: 'You know something Rob, you were framed! I am certain someone has cut the ropes, and attempted to harm you? Jesus Rob, you lucky to 'be alive? Back then you would end up be dead cold, if your Boss did not swap the rope with you? Have you got enemies, which have wanted to hurt you?'—They sit hushed. Rob look be lost at sea: 'I didn't think this way, before? I knew dudes who hate me a lot?'—Rob hesitates; then tells more: ' . . . I was convicted, caused by the case. After I was unable to find a decent job! For that reason I arrive here to start over?'—Dan slaps Rob over his shoulder: 'Rob don't worry about it, you will be okay.'—Rob's panting; and is reacting: 'I hope so mate? Now, I have a job on a bid for you, Dan? And I need a partner, someone I can trust in every part of my dealings'—Dan thinks for a bit; and raises his head up; he then ask out of curiosity: 'Really? What type of job do you have in mind, Robert?'—. . . Rob discloses Dan without giving all away; but looks around is wary: 'Well, the job involves finding some rich clients, so as to sell stuff.'— Dan be stunned: 'What kind of stuff? If that involves selling drugs, I am out right now . . .'—But Rob stops him, and sees to it: 'I don't deal drugs, because I abhor that crap! It's a differ deal! The source, where I get stuff from cannot be revealed to you. And you must not seek to get out of me! Dan will you back me up on it, or not?'—Dan shakes with his upper arm; raises up eyebrows, and he winks. On a happy note Dan nods his head: 'I will see, what I can do.'—

Chapter 21

Seen at the University hall of Syracuse has arrived in Nora Lonsdale. By way of rushing she is unbuttoning her fur-coat by now, then gave to one of that stuff to be hanged it up.

Suddenly Martin's shows up aside, as his eyes peek Nora, and start glowing, as he is staring at her. Martin instantly verges upon her in sweet talks: 'Good evening! Are you not early for the lectures, Eleanor?'—Of a silly shock Eleanor turns to glimpse at the person, and her reaction: 'Good evening! You have scared me on coming from behind! I recall now, your name is Martin, is it not?'—Now Martin glows; and politely: 'Yes, I am Martin! May I ask if you have special plans for tonight?'—She feels awkward: 'In fact I do have plans for tonight. And, call me Nora!'—She hesitates to say more; and bows her head down: 'I came here earlier, for a meeting with someone! Sorry if you . . .'—He appears being forlorn: 'Is your meeting about the Law course? Who is this person?'—But Eleanor has prevented him from talking; like so she is definite: 'My meeting has nothing to do with study! It's a private affair!'—But Martin tries cling one-to-one: 'Is that so? This is someone I know?'—On the spot Eleanor is forlorn: 'I doubted! His name is Robert, and he is studying in our College! Else, he came from Detroit. Once I helped him to find housing!'—His eyes glow dies off Martin, as he looks in disbelieve: 'Who do you say it was? Is his surname not by any chances to be Lipinski?'—Now Eleanor seems is stunned, and nods her head logically, but snaps: 'It's him! He and I are meeting tonight!'—Martin's face in a flash alters to pale; seen his entire body is begun shaken. Nora contrary in disparity; as is kept of talking: 'Do you know him, Martin?'—Hot on the heel, he tries keeping composure; even if it hurts, and he felt be like a loser: 'As a matter of fact, I do!'—Nora stops him, she looks being stunned, thus is asking him over: 'Really? How this came about?'—Now he saw a chance to break up Nora and Rob: 'Nora, is you interested to uncover all about him?'—Her upper-body is shaken, and is panting; she then sees to: 'What is to know about Robert?'—Martin schmoozes; as he is keen: 'I will tell you about him! It's up to you to make out your mind?'-

CHAPTER 22

All but a year or two have passed. At the present has past mid-night. Seen it's winter outside with plenty of fluffy snow-white all-round.

Here comes into the view Rob, who is held tight Eleanor, while they have exited a Disco club. To glance this girl is too drunk thus hardly walked being unbalanced; seen Rob is leading the way? She yells pronto; and in one goes, laughs: 'Rob, why you're holding me? Let me go?'—She tried to be free from Rob's firm hands; but without his help she could easily have a fall and get hurt on icy-road. He beams, feeling nervy is close too her: 'Sorry Nora, but without my help you slip will fall on ice, where you get hurt?'—Rob sees Nora is pig-headed, thus he walks faster; she contrary is amazed: 'Rob, you have amazed me in a flash! Tell me where have you got so much cash to spend?'—Hearing it, he alters to be tense: 'Why do you want to know?'—She amends to talk to him, be pleasant: 'Hi, big spender! Today you paid for my chic gifts; you have wasted money to buy me things that I need to labor for years? Believe it or not Rob, but I 'couldn't earn so much, so as to live in luxury?'—Robert smirks; but looks uptight, when is reacting: 'For your information, Nora, I have a job! I work as a sales consultant. That I need to take trips a great deal . . .'—Nora disrupts him, and says be ironic: 'A sales consultant? Whoa!'— Robert appears be of coyly: 'Yep Nora, today is your birthday, and I gave you gifts since you're worthy of all!'—Now Rob's look as if him be lost at sea: 'You and your family helped me, when I have needed a place to live in? Yet we must have faith since we know each other long enough?'—Nora stares; gave him a smile, and inhales; then she tries to cling to his hand undercoat. Her reaction with affection for him, as is certain on one thing: 'Okay! But I wouldn't like being indebted to anyone, even if it's to you, Rob? I have found a good job?'—Arising as hears Nora hiccups; and Rob glows. But she told be impulsive: 'As I was saying, I trust you won't insist on, you know what I meant?'—She winks; and is pointing her eyes below his stomach, so as to attract him. Now Rob began laughing; and is shaking his head; he then answers back: 'Nora, look me in the eyes . . .'—He stops short. She pulls up her chin to look in his eyes. He contrary, curtsies his head; is taken her hands in his, and strokes them ardently: 'Do I give the impression of someone that will insist you know on what thing? Yes, I have paid for gifts as thanks to you! Now, do not distress yourself about it? I give you're my word, Nora!'-

Just now he saw a taxi that has stopped near their stand. Hot on the heel, Rob began running toward the cab. Next he is dragging Nora along, and him being half-embracing her on the way to a taxi.

Moments later Rob opens taxi door, and quickly pushes Nora in the cab; then alone is seated near her, at the back sit of the car. Inward, the taxi driver rotates, and is facing the duo: 'Where would you like to go?'—Rob raises his head up, and gave direction to the driver; he then leans up front near this man, and engages: 'Hey man! Can you drive us to, she is a bit drunk, and it's her birthday! I will pay you double, speed up! And listen, driver, can you close your windowsill, please? Give us some privacy, will you?'—The driver winks, has agreed; he then is shutting car-window, and sways across sheet of glass inward. Rob meanwhile, shifts closer to Nora's ears, at the same time as he half-whispers into it, as his lips is touching her earlobe. When next he spins, and is facing her; he pointed: 'So, what did you want to know about me?'-

Later that night, Rob and Nora are walking outside the cottage, where he dwells. Pronto he lifts her up; and is carrying into bedroom. When he is trying placing her under bedding; instead she enchantingly has grabbed him by his jacket. Her be sly; and drawn near him so as to kiss he's lips. As being enchanting she tries for persuading:—Tell me, why you were good to me? It's because you're owed me? Rob Lipinski, how it's possible to figure you out?'—Just as he speaks is frank, and behaves like a real gentleman: 'Nora, you drank more than you can handle! You will regret, what you're intend to do, here! Don't look at me like that it is true? Be a good girl, and go to sleep! Okay, Nora?'—Just then she grabs Robert by sleeve, and drags him in bed on top of her; still her being charming: 'Yeah? You did buy me chic gifts! Though I'm not that kind of girl, who goes in bed with a complete stranger, which she just has met?'—Her breathing deepens: 'But, in my case I do like you very much, Robert! Why we haven't done it before, you know what I mean? Don't you like me? Spill it out?'—Rob appears be faint-hearted; but has concealed his attraction to her, even if he nods, as is charming:—Oh, I would be a fool not to like you!—Yet Nora tries undressing him. Rob instead is firm to her demand: 'Nora, stop it! Listen to me! Today I want to buy you gifts, since you have lent me a hand in hard times! But, later you will regret, what you're prepared to do! Nora, come back to your senses?'—He's resultant: and tells her a tale about himself, without given away the whole story . . .

Just a bit of time pass, since this pair heads be put together. Rob strokes her hair: 'Are we threw with mix-up, and wrong ideas of yours, Nora?'—She beams so as to attract him again: 'Yeah! But don't you want to have me, Rob?'—Robert is struggling by temptation: 'Enough! Go to sleep! I will cover you up! There you are! Good night, Eleanor!'-

Rob then covers her with a blanket; gets up of her bed. As a respect he has switched off the light, and is leave-taking the room at once.

CHAPTER 23

Since the friendship between a teen and a magpie started, Rob's partner in crime Gale would fly around many regions, usually in the hours of darkness. Accessibly for a bird that is kept raiding well-located homes, without folks are near.

Once upon a time at far-flung is nighttime. Now came into the view a two-store villa someplace in the countryside, whereas on upper floor light is on, and the balcony wide-open. What is anticipated that the house owner of is not home at this time?

From nowhere a magpie has flown, and is landing on a cornice of that house. Initialed Gale turns it's tiny neck around, and glanced through the zone. After the magpie swings with its wing, and cries out; then is flown in; seen it is landing on the surface of a dresser, whereas a jewelry box be, and the owners kept accessories. The bird began unlocking box without key to the locker, and has used its beak. A magpie open bony beak employs its, and succeeded; then in few attempts is able to pick up one-by-one of sparkly jewels. Observing Gale has thrown one by one jewels into a teeny bag that hanged down from its tiny neck. Once Gale has done working, it takes off up; then the bird is flown through an open balcony, who know where too.

Advancing, by en route Gale cries out: Kar-Kar!'-

The magpie is soaring for extensively since it has left that place.

By crow's next airlift, seen it is landing up on a Christmas tree's branch, located in the forests.

Briskly the crow closes her eyes it sounds that Gale is asleep. Only if tomorrow dawn the bird is flying far, en route, destined for Rob's bungalow.

The next day, magpie is up in the air for a while. A crow flew with intervals, and has in its control a hefty bag that hanged down from bird's tiny neck.

Now its hour of darkness. Seen Rob strolls; then laid-back, he stops on the threshold. Be assured that no one heard; Rob exits. Then without delay he is climbing the staircases; and end up on the loft.

Inner Rob silently pushes out, where a way into the loft is; and the door gets open. Candidly, for Gale hearing Robert steps climbing to loft, where magpie is seated up on small roof of a Dollhouse. Given a tiny bag be hanged from bird's neck, which hasn't been filled with much weight that it can carry. Rob gave a grin; and talks in slogan: 'So did you bring something exciting today on your wings, Gale?'—The Crow is responding: 'Kar! Kar!'—As Rob approaches the magpie; he then began at once taken off from bird's neck out this bag. Next Rob is seated down on stool; and arranges small-scale of jewelry that, be wrapped in a plastic bag. He fancy: as seems is estimating its value: 'I guess it's not a lot here, Gale? I must go to get the rest of stuff from somewhere!'—The Crow respond with: 'Kar!'—Here Robert waits, after picks up a rucksack, and exits attics without delay.

Later that night Robert's van is accelerating through highway. Beside him being seated Dan Ming that is in the front sit.

Moments later the truck turns off main road, then it drove toward a zone be out-of-the-way.

Soon the crow croaks, as gives to the duo a signal from above: 'Kar!'—Advancing the bird is landing on top of a tree that roofed with wide branches.

In next to no time the van breaks on the brink of riches tree. As those two getting out of the car, are looking around, but both careful. Dan be nervy:

'Are you sure it's the right place to stop, Rob?'-

Robert raises his head up to observe the area: 'I am sure, Dan, look up on that tree?'—He points a hand up: 'Can you see up over there is seated Gale!'—Dan looks up on a tree: 'Okay mate, if you say-so? Who's going to climb the tree?'—A Robert talk is in biting wits: 'If you're so afraid of heights, Dan? I guess I will do it, myself?'—Rob is pursuing, when checks his jacket pockets: 'Where is my torch?'—Dan endows him with a torch: 'There you're, Rob. Be careful?'—Rob picks up a backpack, and fixed it on rear of his back. As he clings to a torch that is held in his hand; and began climbing the tree. By now he is advanced up to its peak.

CHAPTER 24

Surprisingly in Lipinski's house the telephone is ringing. At the moment Hugo rests on the futon and is watching television. He gets up of his sit, and lazily answers the call: 'Hello, Lipinski residence!'—While, on the phone line in a cottage, Rob is listening eager to step-father's voice. But his voice alone is tense, when spoke on the phone: 'Hi, Hugo! It's me, Rob!'—In Hugo's voice is felt zeal: 'Oh hi, Rob! How are you doing, son?'—Hugo is not got the sense of hearing what Rob tells him. So Hugo is kept talking: 'It's good to hear your voice? We are all okay. Little Randy is all grown up, daily bit-by-bit!'—As Hugo listens to Rob; sudden his face changed faintly to pale; and so his voice is edgy, when he snaps: 'For God's sake Rob, no! How I will explain my absence to Rosy that, I have to take a trip?'—Rob has told a story; and Hugo is resultant: 'Fine! I will do it. I will meet you halfway up there, okeydokey? See you later, son!'-

Chapter 25

Here be seen a big sign: Welcome to Mexico! It's time of spring in Mexico City, where the climate warm, and the nature is blooming everywhere you go.

Now came into sight Rob, who does a prompt delay; as he steps out of the car.

A sun-ray has caught Robert by surprise, and is blinding him up in a flash. Beside him, be spotted Hugo that seated in the car's front sit, seen he's being tense.

A moment later Robert ascends stairs in the Hotel, to where Hugo has driven them both all the way . . .

Curtly passing through the sliding doors, Robert is drawn near that fancy reception desk.

Just as Rob dials a number on his mobile, and is telling someone over the telephone in a calm voice:

'Hi, it's me! I came as planned!'—Robert listens warily to a man's voice on other side of the line.

A strange man's voice on phone answers: 'Okay, did you come in a cab?'—Now Robert talks on the phone:

'No, but you can say that!'—A strange voice is responding: 'Well then, come upon floor five, to suite 18? Guest is waiting just as we speak'—Rob bows head down; and looks at his wristwatch, is shown there: 11.08 a.m. By the local time-zone.

An hour later in a hotel-suite saw Rob that, be seated among businessmen. Beside him, it brings to attention two foreigners, one who are Japanese man, Nakimuro. He doesn't speak English; so these rests are gathering around and having brought a Japanese translator, who is present. Be observed a reaction amid those parties under pressure. Sudden one among is swaying his hands up; seen these rest of that company having wondered. The translator turns see to a client: 'Mister Nakimuro wants to ask if? . . .'—

With translation being made on valuation for the client, guess how much he should pay for Rob's goods? He then spins back see to that party: 'How much do you expect for the lot?'—Rob looks at this client, who with self-confidence talks softly, but he is strict: 'I want you to pay in $US Dollars!'—The interpreter turns translates back to the client that in his turn bows, but is shaken his head: 'Mister Nakimuro says he needs time out?'—

Be heard Grandfather's clock banged: and it's shown time: 15.48 p.m.

Soon the Japanese client returns, only is explaining via the translator. Seen him ducking his head, be shaken with shoulders; but his body language shown he is given a consent. The translator nods his head down and up: 'Nakimuro agrees! But the price you insist on is more than he has estimated to pay for that stuff?'-

Then the translator takes in hand it, and Robert at last seals the deal.

CHAPTER 26

Long times pass. At the present meet Martin, who has walked in the Interpol's center, in New York. Seen he sits down in a chair of sets at the lobby. Here came into the view the two men are wearing civil suits, as they stood aside. By way of looking at each other, next to Martin, they're amused; and pass winking. By acting, Martin looks around.

Eventually he gets up of his sit, is getting ready to embark on a certain one in windowsill. There in he's spotted an officer that is active on a case . . .

Fifteen minutes later Martin has entered a lift to go up on that aimed office, while one of the men winks at him, and is telling to another: 'Cyclops has revived and returned?'—View as those two that wore suits, are begun laughing their heads off.

Martin is remained in Interpol's HQ; when gets out of elevator. He at once has found that office. Next he looks around, and is pleased: 'I am on level six. Here is suite-166, and it's Chief's office?'—Martin's walking to be aimed office, as seeming is panic-stricken. Before entering, he began knocking at the door.

Briefly, inner bureau seen a man be in command, an Interpol's team expert, this is inspector Colubrine that is emerged in his late thirties; and has black-haired. Colubrine wears on a dark suit; and he is engaged talking on the phone to someone. Thus, he doesn't hear that Martin is outside his door, and knocked. Just then he saw, him be busy: 'I will take care as it happens! It didn't click to you, what I have just said?'—Resulting he listens to a voice on the phone, who told him something important. Next he's responding:' As it's ensued then?'—The inspector listens; takes breathes; he then raises a worry over the phone:

'Okay, I will do, what I can!'-

Second knock. At this time Colubrine calls:—Yeah?

Who is there? Come in!'—Martin opens a bulky door; and budges, is walking toward a desk, where inspector be seated. He then sits down, without be invited. Colubrine comes across to him; but being unable to make up his mind about Martin: 'Who are you? Why are you here?'—Martin has avowed as if he is shy: 'Sir, I came for the reason that I want to work here!'—Colubrine in his turn smirk, looks at him; and shakes with his upper-body: 'Why? What forced you do it?'—Martin in contrast, is dazed: 'I don't follow your question, Mister?'—Colubrine is firm; but in quirk of fate:—Lad, for you're, inspector Colubrine!'—Breach in speech: 'Merde! Don't give me a shit talk! What's the real reason you're so eager working in Interpol?'—He hits Martin's ego, who is stern: 'Inspector, I wish to tell you about me!'—Colubrine stops him; conveys it seemingly is snooping: 'You didn't tell me your name, for a start to make contact?'—Martin appears be lost: 'My apology! My name is Martin McDermott to your services, sir!'—Martin turns his damaged eye by way of facing Colubrine, as inspector has spotted defects on the lad's visage via drops of light. Just now both shut up. Next Colubrine points a hand on Martin's defects, and is ironic: 'I see you have got imperfections? I don't think you capable to handle a risky situation under pressure? 'Else, you're not familiar with jargon amid forces?'—Martin's ugly face turn pale; instead his eyes are shined with anger: 'First and foremost, I have not come here to be insulted? Secondly, you're

not the only one, who made a laughing stock out of me?'—Now
he is breathless but fretful: 'Lastly, I want to have a career, and get
promoted to high ranks in Interpol?'—Martin points a hand on
his defects for chief to see; and he snaps at him: 'Chief, someone
harmed me! Since then, I have chased him long enough! Cause he
is a thief, so I need evidence that young Lipinski is guilty? I want
to put him, where he belongs, in jail!'—They are looking at each-
other; next inspector gave a smirk; as to break peace, he inhales:
'McDermott, you alike Alexander The Great, deviously you like
to win, don't you?'—Paradox: Martin beams, seen his reaction be
self-assured: 'I want to be likely the Victor!'—This time Colubrine
smirks; nods his head; and slaps over Martin's upper arms: 'This is
the spirit we need here! Consider to be hired, Martin?'—Martin
bows head gladly. Inspector then turns conversation to anew
course: 'Now McDermott, tell me more! What is the name of
this crook?'-

CHAPTER 27

View violet twilight that has covered the city through with grey clouds.

Be in the room, Martin injected himself with a syringe. Thus have created an effect on him, which caused figment of Martin's sick imagination. Sudden appearance with a accent of Javert that tuned in, and is talking to sort the lad out: 'So, Martin you couldn't talk sense into the girl?'—Martin nods his head, as is timid: 'No! How could I? Now, Nora won't talk to me!'—Javert's image tries to encourage:—Oh, come on! Don't give up, man! Did you learn how it was in my book? Whir I did all those tricks to an escaped convict, Valijean was hoping one day bring him to Justice?'-

Martin thinks a bit; then ducks his head: 'Oh, yea! In the book all be explained! I follow all like it's in 'Le Miserable'?'—Javert gave a smirk; and slaps over lad's shoulders; he then is re-trying: 'Now it's time to do unforeseen about this Rob? With a big deal, my boy . . .'—

A sudden French inspector has vanished. Martin stood randomly in doubts; as he is mad; and revising what Javert has told him: 'I am not sure, what would-be a big deal by inspector's guidance?'-

Involuntary somewhat have struck Martin; that he reflects unwisely: 'You bastard, Lipinski! Because of you I became a laughing stock, and be named Cyclops in that force! My career is going nowhere? Likewise I can't get promoted! Minutes ago this dickhead has married Nora! I will kill him with my bare hands! Unless Rob would get down I swear it!'-

CHAPTER 28

All but three years have past. Here saw layover of darkness.

At this instance sighting Robert, who is walking amid a crowd of passengers in New York's Railway. He stops on the spot, looks around warily. Later, in close proximity Robert has found a public telephone. He watchers around; next dial a number, whereas Rob is heard hum on the phone line. A man's voice answered to his call, is speaking Chinese, this is Xiang's voice on the phone: 'Xiang's restaurant, can I help you?'—Silence on both sides of the line. Promptly a man's voice is switched to English, hearing he talks with an accent: 'Hello, this is Restaurant who is speaking?'—Rob confused, so be on the phone, he inhaled: 'Hello! Is Mister Xiang there?'—A man on the phone listens; then inhales; and came his response: 'I am Mister Xiang, how can I help you?'—Rob is daring: 'Good evening sir my name is Robert . . .'—Xiang prevents Rob from saying, which alone spoken in a sharp voice: 'How did you get my number?'—Rob shuts up. Ensuing he is convincing: 'Dan Ming has given it to me! I would like to meet you, sir?'—Yet Xiang's voice is edgy: 'Where is Dan? I want too see him?'—Rob listens; inhales, and is saying: 'No! Dan is not in New York just now! I hope to show you the goods, mister Xiang?'—Xiang is panting on the phone line, as it's struck him: 'Ah, so? Now I remember! As for the goods my clients want 50% off stock?'—Now Rob is decisive: 'Mister Xiang, this is crazy! I cannot agree . . .'—Xiang cuts Rob short; and is declaring softly: 'When you come to see me, bring Dan with you! Okay?'-

Rob still hangs around Railway; stood aside; he looks around is mindful of that crowd near. All-round the Train Station keen-sighted those crowds of travellers are leaving, or disembarking: as they walk back and forth. Visibly trains, be heard their signals as these pass by.

Meanwhile Rob dialed a number on his cell phone; and began talking on. Whilst saw in a house, Dan's voice is on mobile: 'Hello, Ming is speaking?'—Rob's voice is nervy on the phone:— Hi, Dan it's me!'—As Dan listens on the phone line; and puts a smile: 'Hi, Rob! How's your things going?'—Rob listens is on alert, by taken a deep breath, he answers: 'Not so good! 'But, I am glad to hear your voice, Dan!'—Dan re-joins: 'What is the matter, Rob?'—Rob breathes deeply: 'I called to your link, but it didn't go well as I thought it would?'—Dan on the phone line listens; breathes in a tense voice: 'What seems to be the problem?'—Rob retorts: He offered me price not as I have hoped! Those clients want half price for a heap? You know a right value for it, Dan?'—The two on both sides of the lines are breathing; while they deep in thoughts. Now Dan's voice alters to be edgy: 'What was the man's reaction? Could that seal the deal?'—Robert here listens wary; he then breathes deeply into the phone: 'He's said that can pass the clients a massage! He wants you to come along? So, Dan can you find me new clients, you know how to!'—Those two on both phone lines are panting. Rob puts one hand in his pocket, and inserts a bag be wrapped in fabric. He stares at a bag, as talks, yet being deep in his thoughts. First Dan is mumbled: 'Rob! Wait a minute, why I need to be in New York? Can you settle the deal alone?'—Yet Rob is tense: 'No, it's because the client fancy big profits?'—Dan is wary: 'This all thing be odd?'—Dan shuts Rob up; while is rasping; and he states: 'Then again, if you come to the clients behind Xiang's back, you will end up in jail? Rob, you must agree too Xiang's ultimatum . . .'—

Though Ming doesn't have a clue that someone bugged into his phone, is intend tapping his telephone, at the same time as Dan, has spoken with Robert. While on opposite side from Ming's house be spotted a van. Soon after in the room upstairs, Dan has ended the call. At the same time in the van two people are sighting as listening to it, and wore on earphones. Be revealed one of them is Martin-Cyclopes, who in earpieces listening eager to a phone conversation of this duo. Once the call has ended; Martin takes off his headphones; and turns in front of another, like is looking excited. Now he makes a call to someone, hears himself talks into a car phone, and Martin's voice is with joy:—Chief, we have got this bastard, Lipinski, at last!—Colubrine is on the phone line listening wary; next he reacts, as his voice is firm: 'Did you track his location?'—The Chief and Martin listen to each-other, as they are breathing. Re-viewing all, Martin is eagerly saying: 'Yes, chief! I gave you my word, didn't I?'-

PART IV

CHAPTER 29

Now is a wonderful morning that bathed in sunlight. Rob stood near a metal gate, and is waiting eager for it gets ajar so as to be released from Jail.

Once Rob far-out of prison's exits; he does make a stop; glance around; then came within reach of Dan, who on happy occasion, is put a smile. He hugs Robert, and slaps his upper body: 'I am glad to see you be free, Rob!'—Robert too is hugging Dan, and does likewise; then made a grin, as he's embracing Dan: 'Me too, Dan! Let's get out of here?'-

Next they are getting into a cab that has been requested, as it's waiting aside.

Later Rob alongside Dan has boarded a local train.

Once train's signal is heard, this duo with other travelers is departing from that Rail Station.

In next to no time both are seated in a carriage, where Dan and Rob are relaxing; flanking, as stared in glass-sill. They are traveling through the city interminably; seen Rob's enigmatic in his thoughts.

By dusk Rob onset, as is rushing across gates way in park, where some empty plants have emerged been arranged on turf, to keep them off frosty climate.

Saw Rob on path, where way in the park, as he is walking solo. At one stage he stops only by the gate to observe, and be wary. In split seconds, Rob decides calling on magpie, which he does in rhymes, for Gale knew it . . .

Whoosh: and the magpie appears, is soaring to his stand. Rob seems is gloomy: 'Hi there, Gale! Sorry, I didn't come before? Such unlucky few days I was having because I was arrested . . .'—He observes magpie, as it seems Gale recognizes, what he has said. Above all the bird is content, as its tiny head and beak be shaken up down. A crow's cry be heard: 'Kar-kar!'—Rob enlightens Gale with tale: 'The policemen were detained me for seventy two hours!

'Thank God, the Cops have not found yet evidence to throw me

in jail?'—He takes a deep breathe; seen as his upper-body and

head are shaking: 'If the Cops had got proof, then I will be jailed

for a long time? All thanks to Martin-Cyclops, no doubt this is

his doing, since he wants 'to hurt me badly?'—Rob then raises

head up, as his right hand signs to a tree: 'Gale, you're my partner!

Show me the way, where jewels be located?'

Afterward Rob bows head down, and is dialed number on his

cell phone; on other side of the line Nora's lovely voice answers:

'Hello! Who is there?'—Rob listens eagerly to his wife's voice;

then he spoke: 'Nora, it's me! I am free!'—Where on the phone

line Nora is wheezing, and is crying.

The moment Robert terminates his call; he spins to face the

bird that has observed him. He too watches for Gale's reaction,

given that bird is aerial. Seen the bird has landed; and by now is

seated on tree's branch. A bird's tiny head spins around, and it's

wary. The crow stares with green eyes at a human, as is moving

up and down its tiny neck. Gale cries, as its echo is heard around:

'Kar!'—Rob ducks his head; and sucks in air. Follow-up, as Rob

runs off.

CHAPTER 30

A few days have passed since Robert's release.

At one night Rob rides in a taxi through New York. After he has left the taxi; and is kept walking ahead. By turning around the corner, he strides across Downtown. Shortly he steps at the heart of Chinatown.

Before long he walks in a Chinese restaurant that Xiang's owned.

Inner Rob saw Dan, and he stops. Rob is eagerly made the way to his table.

A waitress that served tables has approached Rob and Dan; seen her head being down in courtesy for the guests, but she spoke English in an accent: 'What would like to order?'—Rob looks at her; to keep on, his letting her knows: 'I am in the mood for the most delicious meals you have on menu?'

Ensuing, Xiang's merged, and intrudes: 'Do you wish instead, to eat for a special price?'—Xiang tilts his head that is a sign for the waitress to leave. Dan nods his head; Rob contrary seeming is lost at sea; and bows his head in courtesy: 'Nice to meet you at last, Mister Xiang, can we talk privately?'—Xiang in his turn, smirks: 'Ah, so! Let us go upstairs, then? It will be more comfortable up there . . .'—

Up-to-the-minute view upstairs is a typical hidden room. This is where Robert sits down at the table beside Dan, and where on other side seen Xiang. Rashly Rob puts a hand in his pocket, and removes a bag be wrapped in fabric. He has untied, and laid it over the table, and they are looking on collection of jewelry, which contained a quantity handy. Those three are amazed; and as one curve their heads, then over to view goods. Xiang cling to the heap so as to look at it closer freely, and is addressing Dan in a cool voice: 'How much does he wants for stack?'—Rob take aback; and saw a chance to raise the price up. He puts a grin; says be cocky: 'In pile real jewels! Before moving on the lot, we need to agree on its value? Am I wrong, Dan?'—Here Rob keeps them from talking. Dan nods his head up and down, is favoring. Suddenly Xiang gets up of his sit; as he is with a greedy nervy grin: 'Excuse me, please, gentlemen! But I have to think about it?'—Xiang then quits the upstairs room, and is closed the door quietly.

As Xiang reappears at last, is footing, and rubbing his left hand with his right. He thinks for a bit; then states:—Your name is Robert?—Rob nods head and smiles; saw he's eyes sparked: 'Okay, let it be 'your way! I need to look in depth on goods that, you should know how dealing be done here, and in other places?'—He then looks at Dan, who nods to go-ahead: 'Of course I agree, sir!'—Xiang bows his head; and inserts a magnify glass to look closer on jewels, which are sparking, laying here: 'Okay! All is settled then?'—All at once Dan signs to Rob that embarks to, and mumbled is coy: 'Mister Xiang, Dan told me of your connections? So, I want to ask if . . . Well, I have a secret thing to ask of you?'—Xiang is amazed: 'Ah, so? What kind of secret thing?'—For Rob is seemingly awkward; so he has hesitated to spill out, being nervy; at last he states: 'Sir, I am under microscope? I awfully need a valid ID with new names? Can you help? If you can't, just forget about this talk between us?'—This Chinese man smirks; as he has guessed, being crafty: 'So, Rob your surname is Lipinski?'—This duo nods their heads, jointly. Xiang ducks his head; it seems he is agreed to do dealing: 'You come to the right place! And, yet if 'you want our deal to be sealed we have to compromise, then? If you agree to do for me a deal?'—Rob look be dazed: 'What type of deal? Sir, what is it you want me to do? I am not a crook!'—Xiang signs with his eyes on riches, which lying upon the table: 'You two 'bring me a bag with diamonds, whereas in port ship container is. It's to be delivered from Russia?'—Yet Rob is alarmed, and apt to ask: 'How I am infer to know, in which port?'—Xiang is casually: 'I will let you know, when goods are delivered! Now, what will you do? Are you agree to do big business?'—Rob looks at Dan, who nods; and Rob re-joins: 'Dan and I have to think about?—Saw Xiang is crafty: 'If you will give me price cut on goods, Robert? And, I will agree to find you ID!'-

CHAPTER **31**

It's a nighttime came. Given Rob is in the house that, sitting on bed's corner. Beside him is Nora, who seems being distressed to cry. So Rob strokes her hair, is decisive: 'Nora we must decide now since we go away, before it is too late?'—Eleanor takes a deep breath; lifts her head up; she appears be lost at sea: 'Why we need to leave, Rob? Do you 'plan for an escape to happen soon?'—Except for Rob, who is jumpy: 'I am afraid so! It's essential that you're, Nora accepting my plan?'—Nora thinks for a bit; and tells him of her opinion; but she is grim: 'I wish we were not rushing things?'—Yet Rob stops her; shakes his head, as if he has disapproved. Spur-of-the-moment he tries to clear up for her lovingly, but urgent: 'You're wrong! Nora, back me up on it? Cyclops is after us! We don't have a choice? So, I beg you to be patient? I have it all under control, babe?'-

Following the pair began passionately kissing. Arising both is getting undressed steadfast. They're going with the flow; seem both desperate; Rob utters: 'I love you, Nora!'—She re-joins: 'I love you . . .'—

Slowly they are sliding over bedding, A full moon excels via the window.

Meet a crow is in mid-flight. Intuitively inn lovemaking has developed between this pair of loving birds; while Gale outside, began crying out.

CHAPTER 32

J ust now is nighttime in San Francisco, where a Shipment a minute ago has docked into the Seaport.

Up-to-the-minute this ship has disembarked goods on shores; seen a sailor among that crew nearby; as he looks around, be edgy. This sailor is delivering the goods, when opens container's door, and takes out enfold. He has moved; and swaps item for spare one, he seems is like 'a cat on a hot tin roof'.

At this point on highway came into the view a van be driven toward the Port. Seen the van's driver spins, and does a U-turn. Progressing, the truck stops near, and close to the way in that Port.

In next to no time in the Port, saw Rob stood beside Dan is talking with the sailor. Hear the sailor speaks Russian: 'I have brought you goods?'—Rob looks at Dan, but both don't understand him: 'Listen comrade, do you speak English?'—The sailor stares at those two; and nods his head; he then began talking English in a brogue:—Yes I do. I have said here are the goods!'—Next the sailor inserts out of his pocket a bag is wrapped in fabric, and shows it up: 'There you're! Now, how 'will you pay me for the goods? I risked my neck, to bring these stones in US?'-

Robert instantly opens his case be hanged down from his arm; and shows up to him, what it's in there?

Sailor nods his head, seems he has changed to content.

For the past minutes: money change hands. The main deal being made, once this sailor has exchanged the wrapped riches for Robert's kit.

Later that night Robert is seated alongside Dan in front sit of the car, and has driven that truck. Once Dan turns around the corner; and the van stops near a Chinese Restaurant, where Dan parks it . . .

Rob glances through, be tense: 'Let's go inside?'-

Sees Dan is nervous, thus he looks around: 'Yep! But we have to be careful?'-

In the room upstairs, Rob is seated at the table. Beside him is Dan; on opposite side of the table sat Xiang. Those three are deep into scrutiny the goods, which Rob and Dan have brought prior. Xiang has unwrapped stuff; and reveals unfurl that be packed with gems. This trio is looked with wide-open eyes, and being stunned. Robert looks at ID is amazed: 'So this is your deal for my documents, Mister Xiang?'—Xiang raises head, he's browsed up to see an expression on faces of the two; he smirks; and mutters: 'Yes, can't you see it? My goods real Siberian diamonds! But this is not the end of our deal! Causes the two of you have to deliver half of that pack to those clients? Now I split the goods in-half.'— Saw Xiang sifts gems into a bag; rashly he gets up of his sit, and moves items to a drawer. He then removed a spare bag alike that be wrapped from his pocket. Ensuing he opens cabinet, handles one time a case that doesn't open. Now he is itemized: 'Here is a bag for you and the case!'—He gave kit to Rob. All is stared in silence. Now Xiang insists: 'You both have to cross the bridge, and go to New Jersey to deliver half of goods to the clients? And me bring money?'—

CHAPTER 33

For now is red-blood twilight in the city; weather is cold. On the highway Ming is fast-tracking the truck. Inside the van came into the view Robert, Nora and Dan are sitting therein.

To the police has become known that this trio left the city half-an-hour ago . . .

Suddenly, came from behind a series of those police cars, which are chasing behind this trio's truck.

Given Rob is seated in the front sit of a car that, Dan holds a steering wheel. In van's back sits Eleanor is looking pale and panicky. All of a sudden Robert yells, and his hands waved up in the air: 'Dan, press on gas! The Cops are closing in! Drive, faster!'-

Rooting pro the Cop's auto 'BMW', whereas Martin is seated on the back sit, near Colubrine, in between them the officers, who are too seeing in this car. Rashly Colubrine is yelling urgently: 'Come on man speed up! Or we are going to lose them from view!'-

So far the Police are in the position and ready to shoot. Martin stares from car's window; when says firmly: 'Its emerged be odd, but a risky ordeal for them to escape from us? We'll get them, Chief!'-

Dan senses a disaster: police is shooting from car-window, and carry on firing to their truck . . .

A sudden tailed-chased car came near this trio that has driven off on high-speed. When Robert checks car's speedometer it's shown—85 km . . . 89 . . . 90 . . . and is kept climbing high. In a difficult situation Rob is shouting: 'Dan, press on gas, to a full-speed!'-

Next he turns to see what is going on with Nora. She appears being in poor health, and trembling off fear. Spur-of-the-moment Rob caresses her cheeks: 'What's wrong with you, Nora? Can't you hold on, until we get to Canada? Take breathes!'—As her breathing deepens. Given Nora is on the brink of nausea that, covers her mouth with a hand palm, and talks in a tender voice: 'I wish I knew? I don't feel well! I will try to hold on for you!'—Rob strokes her hair; and holds her in his arms; then bows his head down to rub her hand, and kiss them. Now he is kind: 'I am sorry for getting you in such 'danger, babe?'—Nora looks him in the eyes; and began crying; seeing tears run down her light skin cheeks. Hearing she is sobbing, and panting: 'Despite I wouldn't wish parting from you? Robert, don't you dare give up!'—Quirk of fate, Rob stops her; he is firm: 'It would be better, if I let you get off the van, Nora? So, you won't get hurt 'through terror?'—Rob resulted that, points out with his eyes at Dan to bring van to a halt. It's quick-thinking, Rob opens the door, when has pushed Nora out from the car, outer. Once he locks the car door; and influentially yells: 'Go faster! Accelerate, Dan!'—Since their van being chased, Dan is activating, and speeding up.

In the police car meanwhile, an officer saw Nora be footed on the side road. Martin has spotted her there, and his heart starts pumping. Thus, he feels his breath be caught in, and stares from car-window. Yet he is excited: 'Chief, can we stop for a second?'—Colubrine spins to face Martin; he looks thinking Martin is crazy; so he is angry: 'Why! Have you gone nuts?'—But inspector spins back; and grabs walkie-talkie; when is declaring via radio: 'All listen carefully! Stop your cars near a woman on the side road.

And bring her to talk later!'—An that occasion Martin is blissful: 'Thank you, Chief! Sir, you strike for me a chord of inspector from the book 'Le Miserable'?'—Colubrine spins to the front, and declares be with a stare: 'Cyclops, you know something you're crazier, than I initial thought?'-

Soon the Police and Interpol in back accelerating, as they are chasing in the cars a double act's truck. Next see that force is attempting to catch this duo. Martin is frantic, as he assured: 'Their van is barrelling for the Lakes to jump into Canada?'—He stops; see one of his hand is atop, with a second free he clings to the steering wheel. Colubrine still is jumpy; but has changed his mid; is telling to one officer; and fix your eyes on the road: 'We need to cut off their oxygen!'—Martin is nosy: 'Chief, what's that stands for?'—Colubrine is breathless; while his eyes fixed on the road; and he explains: 'What I have meant is to take action! To cut off their way from all sides: trains, Airport and so on! We have to catch them, and confiscate those goods.'-

Much later convoys of the police cars are pursuing Rob's truck, while pushing them off to a bridge.

Without warning someone from the chased cars opens back car window, and is firing on the tyre of Rob's car. Look-see down on tyre trace is residue of gunshots.

In a difficult situation Dan presses on the footbrake, and avoid to be caught. But a van doesn't stop, as it is in motion, which resulted to domino effect. As a result the police cars have got in a collision with those front pursued vehicles . . .

Other of police cars made attempts to catch Rob's truck that swerves on a critical point. On the spot the van turns sharply sideways, have intent not to be collided speedily into a railway of the bridge fences.

Those vehicles at the front of the chasing convoy are assembled in a row, after having attempted to overtake, and resolved intercept off the speeding van. Robert is edgy, and often tags on Dan's sleeve, but is agitated: 'Be careful, Dan! Speed 'up! Don't stop! Cops are speeding, when chasing us 'in their cars at the rear! They are near us! Dan, stay put of the wheel, quick, press on gas!'-

By late night the police vehicles on Bridge have surrounded Rob's truck. It's resulted for the truck traveling to the frame of bridge's fence. When it has caused for the car foundation slowly shaken, and its structure is rocked. In split seconds the van is gradually fallen down; then the car body hits hard into the water. From the time when they have left, Rob sat beside Dan; but both be scared stiff. Paradox: Rob is rational, as tries to open car's glove box; he then slip out from a tiny bag, and puts it in his pocket. But a sudden blast; it is trailing from explosion! Boom! As the duo have felt from behind an awful blaze. A second blast, and the van is burst in flames, it's huge! Its impact has made resonance be heard. Blasts causing violates off blazes that is grime. Spotted flames have flown up in the air, be located far and wide. Since blast has accrued, flash of light in a blitz; trails, as it's seemingly spit lengthily; trailing is evaporated into a mist. Foundation of the truck is on fire, just as car's engine being destroyed . . .

With dawn arose on the Lakes, where echo be heard around. Seen a flamed truck, while it's ashes spew, and flew into the air. Following the van fell into the water, whereas it has exploded. Sees Rob's car is on fire; that image is grown hazier, lying on all sides of the Lake Michigan . . .

A bit later, Martin moves askew; but it seems being untouched by sympathy to Rob. Instead, his mindset with great joy rather than from a shock.

Now Martin is content, like so gave a smirk, and him talking in cliché: 'Rob, you due to what became of you because you have double-crossed me! Ha-ha!'-

Whilst flying in midair, and hearing the crow is crying out . . .

In split seconds miraculously from under the water on the surface, is flown up those two men's heads.

END OF BOOK 1